Daddy Defends

A Drifters MC Novel

Lucky Moon

Contents

Keep in Touch

Thanks for stopping by!

If you want to keep in touch and receive a **FREE BOX SET** as a thank you for signing up, just head to the link here:

http://eepurl.com/gYVLJ1

I'll shower with you love and affection, giving you **insider information** on my series, plus all kinds of other **treats**.

My regular newsletter goes out once a week, and contains giveaways, polls, exclusive content, and lots more fun besides.

Also, you can get in touch with me at luckymoonromance@gmail.com or find me on Facebook. I love hearing from fans!

Lucky

x o x

PROLOGUE

CLEAR YOUR MIND. FOCUS. Be centered.

Two muscular legs, bent above a strong, upturned body.

As Esmeralda breathed, her legs quivered. Right now, they were covered in pastel pink and mint-green tie-dye Lycra. The toenails were painted — each a different, vibrant color — and there was a cowrie-shell anklet around the right foot.

She cradled her head in her hands, supporting her weight on her elbows, as she visualized the pose she was aiming for. An elegant, tall, inversion. Feet to the sky, head and forearms firmly rooted to the earth. It was a position she hadn't been able to pull off for months.

"Come on, Esme... you can do this." Her voice was strained, full of effort.

Breathe.

Esme tried to be mindful. To smell the sandalwood and sage incense that was burning in the corner. To listen to the hypnotic sound of the Tibetan singing bowls playing through her speakers.

She felt the reassuring texture of her cork yoga mat under her arms as she started to lift her feet, to move toward *shirshasana*: a yogic headstand. Her eyes were closed, she was fully present, and she was almost there.

She could feel her form stretching out, taking up more space as her bent legs began to straighten. Blood flowed from toes to her head and back again. She felt each heartbeat as her body elongated, as she got closer to realizing the pose.

Suddenly, the quivering grew more severe, more pronounced. For a moment, it felt like her whole body was about to topple. There was a burn in her core, a sign of weakness, but she tried to fight through it.

Visualize it. Stay peaceful.

She imagined herself on a cool, shaded riverbank. The sound of a stream, and the tweeting of nearby birds. But there was another sound, too. She felt a spike of anxiety. Losing control of her subconscious, she imagined the chatter of people, all around.

Watching her. Mouths open with shock. Judging her.

Her breath became shallow. Jagged. She felt weakness in her arms, pain in her shoulders.

She screwed up her eyes and shouted, "Stop looking at me!"

Esme tried to use the anger and shame to spur her on, but as she did, her body buckled, and with a hard, dull thump, she tumbled down to the ground.

Sitting on the mat, hands on the ground, she sighed and opened her eyes.

She wasn't beside a gorgeous mountain stream. She wasn't surrounded by gentle grassland or tweeting birds. No. Esme was sitting in the middle of her crowded Hunts Point apartment. It was like a physical representation of her brain.

Cluttered.

Messy.

Unfocused.

On top of a pile of dried laundry was Esme's stuffie: Om Baby.

"Om Baby," she said, crawling over to it. "Why am I so messed up?" Om Baby was a posable bunny-rabbit stuffie with closed eyes and a little pink paci in her mouth. Esme liked to pose Om Baby into whatever position she was working on.

She squeezed her stuffie's tummy, and the speaker in her tummy played a smug-sounding "Om" chant.

Esme was lucky not to have hurt herself in the fall. There was a little pain at the nape of her neck where she'd fallen, but other than that, she was okay.

"What do you think? Should I try again, my yoga bunny friend?" she asked Om Baby, but she already knew the answer. She crossed over to her incense burner and rubbed the red-hot tip of the stick against the cedar-wood case, stubbing it out.

An alarm sounded from her computer. "Time to work, I guess."

Being a yoga instructor took time, patience, and a particular skill that Esmeralda Adams would never, ever have. In order to teach, you have to be comfortable to have a crowd of people look at you.

And that was never, ever going to happen.

Esme threw herself down into the threadbare, sticky office chair which she used to stream in, and grabbed a bite of the sandwich she'd been picking at for most of the day. Then, she punched the power button and waited for her computer to slowly clunk its way to life.

It was ironic, really — she couldn't stand the attention of a group of people in real life, but somehow, streaming to a bunch of strangers online didn't bother her half as much. If she couldn't see them, then — somehow — they weren't really there.

Om Baby perched on the side of her desk, legs up in the air, flaunting just how easy it was for her to pull off an inch-perfect *shirshasana*.

In front of the keyboard, Esme laid out her tarot cloth. It was one of her favorite, favorite things. Night-black velvet, with the phases of the moon printed on it in silver. Each phase had a spot for a card beside it, and a line of text to help with interpretations.

Esme checked the feed of the overhead camera — she'd had to suspend it from the ceiling to get a perfect shot of the tarot cloth. It looked good on screen. Well-lit, in perfect focus.

The second camera was focused, of course, on her.

"Wish I looked as good as the mat," she joked to herself. She'd changed out of her yoga gear, and into something a little more... fan friendly.

The truth was, most of the people who tuned into her tarot card reading streams were more interested in *her* than in the cards. She found that she earned more when she wore less.

She undid an extra button on her vest top, showing a little more cleavage than normal, sighing as she did so.

"This is all your fault, Esme. If you hadn't been fired from Natural Magick, then you wouldn't be having to do any of this."

Om Baby watched, upside-down, without judgment.

"You'd have enough money for rent. You wouldn't have to show your boobies off to strangers on the internet. Everything would be fine."

The job at Natural Magick had been good. She'd given readings to customers and helped with sales and customer service. Trouble was, Esme had never been punctual. Not at all. Routine was not her strong point. Neither was following orders.

Go with the flow. That was more her style.

"Hellooooooooo, my esoteric friends," she said, flashing a wide, white smile to the camera. There were already seventy-four people in the chatroom. People who'd been waiting for the start of the stream.

"Thank you all so much for being here. My name's Esmeralda, and I'm going to read some freaking tarot cards for you guys. The sage is burnt. The offerings have been made. It's time to get seriously, deeply pagan."

People posted funny emojis in the chat. Other people said hello.

Esme took out a deck of cards and prepared to for everything to become clear.

Tarot isn't fortune-telling. No. It's more subtle, more nuanced than that. In a way, it's kind of like a therapy session. You and the cards, working together to dig around in your subconscious, looking for a way to make life a little lighter, for a way to make sense of this messy world we all live in.

"Freya," Esme said, "We've got some big, big energy on this reading." She'd already laid out The Ace of Cups (maybe the start of a new romance?) and The Sun (a positive feeling about the current situation). The next card would help Esme really get to the bottom of this situation.

Before drawing the cards, Freya had sent a question to Esme, and it had been a doozy. *Should I quit my job?*

Esme felt a serious responsibility to the people she was reading for. She was aware that she had the power to influence their lives, and it was not a power she took lightly. She tried her best not to answer questions directly. Instead, she left space for people to answer the questions themselves.

With a flourish, she turned over the top card of the deck, and laid it neatly on the Last Quarter moon diagram.

"Ohhhhhh," breathed Esme. "The Five of Cups. Inverted. Interesting." This way up, the card signified emotional healing, and letting go of sadness. "To me, these cards all seem to relate to new beginnings, don't they?"

Freya, who was in her chat, said: *I've got to quit, right?*

Other chatters gave their opinion. They talked about Freya's options, and the hard road that lay ahead of her. It was a healthy, constructive discussion.

Well. Mostly.

Because at the same time as people joining in with the tarot chat, there were a couple of trolls who kept making lurid comments about Esme's looks.

Admittedly, she did have a striking appearance. She had glossy, perfectly straight, black hair, which hung in a heavy, almost rigid bob a couple inches below her ears. Her eyes were bright green, almost impossibly saturated with color. Her skin was pale, and her body was... generous. She got lots of comments about her curves.

Part of her felt strange about it, but, at the same time, she needed the money that the skimpy outfits guaranteed.

In the top right-hand corner of the screen was the donation target for the stream: a hundred dollars. She'd never make it, of course. The most she'd ever made in one stream was sixty-three dollars, and that was a complete fluke. A bigger streamer had accidentally sent a bunch of their viewers into her channel.

Trouble is, today she *really* needed to make that money.

Her rent deadline for the month was fast approaching, and if she didn't make the hundred bucks, she had no idea what she was going to do.

"Okay, Freya, my witchy friend," she said. "Here's how I see things. We've got the—" but before Esme could finish her sentence, the doorbell sounded. "God damn, Freya, hold tight. Chat, I'll be right back."

But she wouldn't.

"Esme!" standing at her open door was Sophia Ragusa. She was one of Esme's closest friends, and like her, she was a Little. "I'm soooo excited!"

They'd met at an event for the Drifters Motorcycle Club, a society of Daddy Doms who also happened to be extremely intimidating-looking, leather-clad, outlaw bikers. If you hadn't seen them for yourselves, you'd hardly believe it. But honestly, something about the dichotomy between hard-as-nails bikers and super-protective Daddies just *worked*. The guys were cool as heck.

Esme had first connected with the Drifters when Marcus — the ex-president of the club — had booked her to give his Little, Tati, a tarot reading. Tati and Esme had hit it off, and before long, Esmeralda was spending more and more time in the company of some very gruff, very serious bikers.

Sadly, Marcus had recently passed away — murdered by Sophia's father. It was a messy, sad story, and Tati was still recovering from the loss.

Sophia was holding an old-looking, brown, teddy bear. She was a stuffie-restorer by trade and was never seen without one of her vintage soft toys.

"Sophia?" Esme asked, a little confused. She'd normally have been happy to see her friend, but she was right in the middle of her stream. Freya was still waiting for her reading. "Everything alright?"

It was Sohpia's turn to look confused. "I think so. I'm... here for my reading?"

The realization hit Esme like a truck. She'd completely forgotten. Sophia was getting married in a month, and today was the day she was getting a reading to help her think about the future.

Esme had completely forgotten.

She thought back to the moment on the mat when she'd fallen down. Out of balance. Everything was totally out of balance.

"Right! Of course! I knew that, of course. I just meant..." She quickly did up the buttons on her vest top. Suddenly, it didn't feel so good to be revealing as much skin as she was. "I meant, are you good to go now? 'Cause I totally am!" Her voice was about as convincing as vegan cheese.

"I'm good to go," Sophia said, "If you still are? If it's a bad time I can—"

"No, no, no, now's the perfect time!"

The perfect time for my life to fall apart.

She smiled as best as she could, but like everything else, it was unconvincing.

What was the point in fighting against who she was? A fuck-up. There was nothing she could do to change herself. She'd always be useless.

Life is all pre-determined. We're trapped by the people we are.

There was no way that Esme could have remembered her appointment with Sophia.

There was no way Esme could have made the money for the rent this month.

There was no way for her to be anything other than Esme.

Forgetful. Weak. Destined for failure.

Esme wasn't in control of her own life. In fact, she wasn't in control of anything. It wasn't even her fault that she'd failed to do the *shirshasana* earlier. It was fate. All of it.

The reading with Sophia went about as well as could be expected. It was obvious that Esme's heart wasn't in it, but she did her best to seem engaged and insightful, nonetheless. The state of Esme's apartment was shameful — she had to sweep a bunch of old rubbish from the dining room table to make room for the reading — but Sophia was kind enough not to mention it.

"Will I be happy after I get married to Wolf?"

It was a simple question, and was answered by The Empress, The Hierophant and — again — The Ace of Cups. All positive cards. Sophia was delighted to hear that it was going to be a time of growth and blossoming love for her. Esme was happy for her, too, but she couldn't shake the negative feelings that sat on her heart like a fat toad.

As she left, Sophia fixed Esme with a serious look. "Girl," she said, squeezing her friend's hand. "Is everything okay with you? Like, really okay?"

Esme forced a grin. She thought about being kicked out of her flat. She thought about being unable to find peace and focus. She thought about having to flirt with deadbeats online for money. She thought about that terrible, horrible day, ten years ago, the day when fate had taken control and agency had slipped out of her grasp.

"Yep," she lied. "Things are good. Never better."

It was later that night, back on her tarot broadcast, as she considered just ripping off her top in the vain hope that the people watching might donate a couple of bucks, that the tears really threatened to come.

Only one thing stopped them.

She was nowhere near her target of a hundred dollars when the message came through. It was from her biggest fan: TwistOfFate43. Someone who could be relied on to always make her feel better when things started to get her down.

TwistOfFate43: *You're so great, esme. You're more than that, you're special. I believe in you.*

Special.

She wasn't special. She was a fallen leaf, floating downstream. The breeze carried her. The current moved her left and right. And she just let it all happen, because what else could she do?

She finished up the livestream, and that's when the tears came.

CHAPTER ONE

Rainer Ortiz ran his palm across the soft green felt of the table's surface. Not for the first time tonight, he wished he was on his bike, instead of being stuck here.

"You feeling lucky tonight, Rainer?"

Wolf sat across the table, his bright silver hair shimmering under the dim lights of the Den's backroom.

"Luck doesn't exist." Rainer's voice was hard. He knew that he had a tendency of appearing like a humorless asshole, but he also knew that right now, Wolf was doing everything he could to put him off his game.

"That so?" his friend asked, chuckling. "That means if you lose, it's just 'cause you suck?"

Rainer didn't answer. He just looked at his cards again. Truth was, he *did* suck at poker. He was too honest for the game. If he ever did try to bluff, it was as obvious as sunrise. So, he tended to just wait for the big hands, and capitalize on them. Trouble is, everyone in the motorcycle club knew that he played like that, so he ended up losing. A lot.

Never mind the open road. Rainer wished he was back in his garage, finishing the tune-ups to the custom Fathead he was working on. Grease and oil, metal and leather, that's what he craved.

On the table was a two and a pair of Queens. He had a pair of twos in his hand. That made three of a kind, which was good in theory, but the fact that it was a trio of twos lessened its power quite a bit. Now, the chances were th—

"Come on, Ortiz, we don't have all night. The meeting's about to start," Crank interrupted. He scratched his bald head with his cards, obviously trying to play it cool.

The reason they were all here tonight was an important one. Marcus, the previous Prez of Drifters MC, had left a will to be read. His life-partner, Tatiana, was going to read the will out to the whole club, as well as to the Littles associated with it.

It was a big occasion, and the guys had decided to play a hand or two of poker before the big event to settle their nerves. Or at least, *Wolf* had decided to play a hand or two of poker. And seeing as he owned the bar, it had seemed rude to turn him down.

"Alright, alright," Rainer said, struggling to decide.

Should he call, fold, or raise?

He wasn't cut out for this kind of game. Much better to be arm wrestling or playing chess. Something without any chance elements. He liked to be in complete control of a situation.

"Fuck it," he said, pushing all his chips — a hundred bucks' worth — into the center of the table.

"Jesus, you sure?" Baron said, thoughtfully stroking his salt-and-pepper beard.

"You're going all in with a pair of twos?" Wolf took a drink from his tumbler — he was tee-total so there was some kind of alcohol-free botanical brew in the cup.

"This reminds me of the only game of Russian Roulette I ever saw. Now *that* was high-stakes. You ever play Russian Roulette, Rainer?"

Baron asked, playing with a hand-forged blade under the table. "Best way to play Russian Roulette is the best way to play poker. You cheat."

"Just play the fucking game," Rainer said. They were trying to throw him off.

So, they did. Crank and Baron folded, not wanting to match the bet. Wolf, however, after a brief moment of consideration, matched Rainer's hundred-dollar wager. "Go on then, tough guy," Wolf sneered. "Let's see what you've got."

Of course, Rainer lost. Wolf had three Queens — a far stronger hand than his.

"You can't fight fate," Baron commented as Rainer pushed the chips toward a happy-looking Wolf.

"No such thing as fate. I'm just a shitty poker player."

It wasn't much longer before the meeting was due to begin. The whole club had showed up to The Den, the official club bar, to hear the reading of the will. It was pretty much agreed that there would be an announcement in the will of the next club president, and it was also pretty much agreed that it would be Baron.

Only problem was, Baron definitely didn't want to be Prez.

"If it had been six months ago," Baron had shared with Rainer over a drink about a week ago, "I wouldn't have thought twice. I'd have accepted, and it would have been the greatest honor of my life. But, you know, since Molly, things have been different."

Baron had fallen hard in love with a Little from his past, Molly. The two of them had gone through a traumatic experience together, and Baron had vowed to never put Molly in danger again.

"If I did become Prez, I'd be in the firing line. Any enemies of the club would be targeting me first. And that would mean Molly would be in danger, too. I can't take that risk."

It had been decided that if Baron's name was called, there would be a leadership election, which, in Rainer's mind, was no bad thing. Meant that it would be a decision for the whole club, rather than the inclination of one man.

He didn't know who'd make the best Prez, but there was one thing he *was* certain of: it wouldn't be him.

It wasn't that the club wasn't important to him. It was. In many ways, the Drifters had saved his life. He'd joined the club when he'd been at an exceptionally low point in his life. Without the brotherhood of the other members, and the leadership of Marcus, his life could have led him down a very dark road.

But lead the club? Nah.

The President of an MC needed a very specific skillset. Rainer had some of the skills required. He was straight-talking and was well-respected by the other members of the club. He didn't take shit from anyone. He was tough and could even be ruthless at times. But... he wasn't exactly a people person. Diplomacy and deception were not his strong point. Also, he was intolerant of incompetence. Maybe he was impatient, too. And a Prez couldn't afford to be those things.

Overall, Rainer was fine spending time with people, but he was much happier with his hands full of engine parts, and the smell of grease on the air. Nothing like mechanic work to keep you grounded. And when he wasn't working on bikes in his shop, he had another hobby which took up the majority of the rest of his time.

The atmosphere in the Den tonight felt a little somber. Normally, Littles and Bigs would be laughing and joking together. Wolf would be mixing mocktails, and Baron would be waxing lyrical about his latest blacksmithing project. Molly would be arguing with Grip about the particular issue of a particular comic book in which a particular character appeared for the first time. It was chaos. Wonderful, happy, maddening chaos.

Tonight, though, it wasn't like that at all. There was no music. No laughter. Just a bunch of respectfully hushed conversations. Even the Littles were being quiet.

"How long has it been since we scattered the Prez's ashes?" Wolf asked, wistfully. "Fuck, can't stop calling him the Prez. Old habits die hard."

"Three months," Baron replied. Molly was sitting next to him. Most MCs had a strict "no girls" policy at club meetings, but that particular rule was more relaxed at the Drifters. Sometimes, Littles needed looking after, and that was that.

"Still feels like he's here," Rainer said, taking a sip from his bottle.

It was true. Even though it had been a while since they'd said good-bye to Marcus, it still felt as though his ghost haunted the club.

Baron nodded. "I think this'll help. The reading of the will. Gives us a way to carry out his wishes, then get on with our lives."

A hush descended over the bar as Tatiana made her way to the front of the room. She was carrying a sealed envelope.

Poor Tati. She'd noticeably lost weight since losing Marcus, and it looked as though she'd aged at least five years in about as many months. She'd been through hell.

"Drifters and friends of the Drifters," began Tati. "It's so good to see you all. Thank you for being here for Marcus."

There was a smattering of words of encouragement and Tati continued.

"As you know, this isn't a legally binding document. Marcus' official will has already been dealt with. This document though, is about my partner's wishes for the future of the club." She opened the envelope and took out a piece of paper, unfolding it. "Here goes nothing." Then, she read. "My beloved brothers. My sweet, darling Littles. I'm sorry I've left you." Tati's voice wavered a little as she tried to control her sadness. "I hope you've all raised a glass to me already. If not, do it now, you assholes!"

There was a roar of bittersweet laughter around the room, as Drifters smacked glasses together and drank deep.

"Sorry for cussin'," Tati said, then continued. "I'm going to keep this short. I've thought a lot about who I think should become Prez of the club now that I'm gone. We need someone with a cool head, who's always got the club's best interests at heart. We need someone who loves the road, and who's got the courage to help us deal with bad situations when they come up — and they will come up." Tati's eyes widened as she read ahead. She looked straight at Rainer. "With all of this in mind, I nominate Rainer Ortiz to be the next President of the Drifters."

There was a gasp, and everyone's eyes turned to stare straight at Rainer.

Ho. Lee. Fuck.

It was late, and Esme was a little, teeny, tiny, itty-bitty bit drunk. Just a smidge, though. Just an absolutely minuscule amount drunk. Like, less than one percent.

"Esme?" It was Sophia's voice.

"That's me!" Esme replied, barely slurring her words at all.

"Are you okay, sugar? You look a little bit confused."

Esme giggled. "Confused? I'm not confused. I'm deadly certain about it all!"

Another Little, Julia, laughed, asking, "What is she even talking about?"

Sophia didn't join in the giggling. "This is meant to be a kind of serious evening, kiddo."

It was true. This *was* a kind of serious evening. Esme had been a good girl up until after the big announcement of Marcus' choice for a successor. Then she'd been a very, very naughty girl.

She was still reeling from the announcement. Marcus had chosen Rainer. Mister serious. Mister "I don't have time to laugh." Mister "I'm irritatingly perfectly proportioned." Mister "My arms are thicker than the trunks of most young trees."

Esme tried to look extremely sober. "Don't worry, Tati told me I was allowed to have fun."

That was also true. After she'd read the will, Tatiana had command-ed that the MC have a good time, celebrating Marcus' legacy, and his contribution to the club. Considering he'd founded the club in the first place, it was a long legacy.

There had been stories about his legendary riding and his bravery. There had been stories about his wise choices and the way he'd led them back to their home in New York City. And there had also been lots and lots of drinking games.

Esme didn't normally drink much. But with the week she was having, and how sorry for herself she was feeling, she couldn't help it. When Sophia had asked if she wanted to share a cocktail with her, obviously she'd said yes. Then she'd said yes to another, and now, she was halfway through a third.

"What do you think?" That was Fleur, one of the only Littles associated with the club who was actually *into* motorcycles. "About Rainer?"

"He's an asshole," Esme said, a little too loudly.

"Esme!" Sophia said, in shock.

"It's true. He's always like 'Esme, don't put your hand near the angle grinder!' and like, 'Esme, five cookies is too many cookies.'" She shook her finger in an accusing way, just the way Rainer did.

"He said that to you?"

"Yeah, I went to his workshop with my scooter one time. Something broke on it. The... fume... pipe? He fixed it, and he showed me the tool he used and gave me cookies."

"Sounds like a monster," Sophia said, sarcastically.

"Exactly!" Esme said.

"I think he's gonna be a great Prez," Fleur said. "He's smart and thoughtful."

For some reason, a flame of jealousy flared up in Esme. Did Fleur have a crush on Rainer? And why did it matter if she did?

"Well, he hates me, anyway," Esme said. "Only four cookies. Pah! Who doesn't eat five cookies?!"

"He didn't look thrilled by the announcement," Sophia said. "Maybe there's gonna be an election after all."

"I don't wanna see Rainer's election," Esme said, stressing the *l* in the word.

The other girls round the table laughed.

"I wouldn't mind," Fleur joked.

Esme felt a tide of nausea rising in her tummy. Was she actually going to vomit?

"'Scuse me," she said. "Just gotta go... somewhere."

She stood up and looked toward the bathroom.

You can do this, Esmeralda. You can make the epic journey to the bathroom.

She looked down, concentrating hard on her feet.

"This is easy. Babies can do it. Well, toddlers. One foot in front of the other." It felt as though the floor was doing its best to avoid her footsteps. "Stay still!"

Esme lurched forward, doing everything she could to stop herself from crashing down into a heap. But as she did, she hit something, hard. A wall of muscle and bone. There was a thump and the sound of glass smashing, and she started to fall forward, but a massive hand caught hold of her arm and pulled her upward, saving her from a world of pain and fragments of jagged glass beneath.

Wait. Why was she so wet?

Not an accident. Not here. Not now.

"Babygirl? Are you alright?"

In a drunken daze, she slowly looked up. Erk. Rainer.

His black vest was soaking wet, slickly sticking to the hard muscle beneath. His arms, stitched with thick, black, biomechanical tattoos, were flexed as he held Esme upright. There was a look of intense concern on his always serious face. A jaw that looked as though it had been hewn from wood, warm brown eyes that burned with fierce, protective energy. Jet black hair, glossy and short-cropped, and a scar over his lip. Ah, his lips. Big and soft-looking, perfect to kiss, to bite, to feel running up and down h—

"Babygirl?"

"That's me."

Esme opened her eyes wide and realized she had spilled two drinks on the floor — well, mostly down the two of *them*.

"I'm sorry!"

"You okay?"

"Peachy. Just wonderfully peachy." The world was spinning and Rainer's perfect face seemed to be filling up her vision.

"You don't seem it."

"Oh, I'm fi—"

And that was the moment that Esmeralda Adams vomited all over the man who'd just been nominated to be the president of an illicit biker club.

CHAPTER TWO

W HEN YOU'RE HUNGOVER, EVEN the most beautiful morning can make you feel as though you're spiraling down into a fiery pit.

"Water. Must... drink... water." Esme's voice sounded like two sheets of paper scraping against each other. She didn't even know where she was or who she was talking to, but she knew that she needed water.

She was sandwiched between tons of blankets. No — sandwiched isn't the right word. She felt burritoed by the blankets, wrapped up safe and warm. If it hadn't been for her unbearable thirst, she'd stay in here all day.

Jesus. What had *happened* last night? She could remember the start of the evening. That part was easy. She'd been with her friends at the Den, toasting Marcus and using booze to forget about the problems in her life.

Then, she'd used a little too much booze, and she had a feeling that she'd ended up giving herself more problems than she'd had at the start. Ugh.

Esme blinked her eyes open. The sun's golden light felt more like the scorching blast from the inside of a volcano against her retina.

"Yowch!" she cried, screwing her eyes shut again. In that moment, at least, she'd got a snapshot of her surroundings. She was in her bed, nice and safe.

"What's up?" The gruff, deep voice shocked her, and she burrowed back into her burrito blanket.

"Who's there?"

"Just your friendly neighborhood puke target."

Puke target?

Oh no. Oh no no no no nonooooo.

The memory was suddenly, painfully clear.

Rainer.

"I'm sorrrrrrry," she whined, feeling more wretched than ever before.

Rainer's face appeared above her. He looked — somehow — even better than he had last night. The golden light of the morning giving his hard face a softness that she'd never seen before.

"Forget it," he said. "We all make mistakes."

"I didn't mean to. I'm sorry. Wait, why are you here?"

"Brought you home."

Slowly, memories swam up from last night's funk. She vaguely remembered Rainer scooping her up and carrying her. Vaguely remembered how strong he'd felt beneath her. Vaguely remembered the whole world spinning like she was on a merry-go-round.

"But why? I puked on you."

"Well, something gave me the indication that you might have been a little bit drunk."

"A little bit?"

"Yeah. Just a touch. Couldn't have you getting yourself into trouble."

"I'm sure I woulda been safe, I j—"

"Pudding, there's no way on Earth that you would have been safe. You couldn't walk. You could barely talk. Yet, somehow, you managed to share your address with me. Anyone coulda taken advantage of you. I had to make sure that didn't happen."

She blinked again, and saw that Rainer was topless. Dumbstruck at the sight of his heavily-inked, thickly-muscled body, she stared at him, eyes wide and mouth agape.

"You okay?"

"Buh buh buh..." she repeated, words suddenly impossible to form. "Brilliant," she eventually managed.

"You want breakfast?"

This was crazy. Rainer Ortiz, a guy who she'd been totally terrified of, was sitting on her bed, checking that she was alright, offering to make her breakfast.

"You're not wearing any clothes."

Why why why did you say that, Esme?

"I am." He got up, showing her his pants. "Tee ain't gonna make it, though. A little too much... fun-juice on it."

Esme felt like she was going to die from embarrassment. She grabbed a pillow and pulled it over her face, before yelling into it at the top of her lungs.

"No need to be ashamed," Rainer said. "It's not the first time I've been covered in vomit and beer. Won't be the last, I'm sure."

"I'm cringing so hard it feels like I'm gonna swallow myself up."

Rainer chuckled. It was the first time she'd ever heard him laugh, and it was surprisingly pleasant to hear. Made him sound almost human.

"That doesn't sound good."

Esme felt a sudden, growing wave of anxiety in her gut. Maybe it was just the hangover, but she couldn't handle this. She felt so dumb, so ashamed of herself. The thought that sensible, serious Rainer was here, judging her, made her feel even worse.

"Rainer," she said, struggling to sound more grown-up than she felt. "I'm grateful for you helping me. But I think I need some alone time now. Try to sort my head out."

"No problem." Was that a look of disappointment on Rainer's face? "And don't worry about last night. In truth, I was looking for an excuse to get away from there. Getting tired of people asking me whether I was gonna be the Prez."

"So, are you?"

He gave her a tired look. "Esme, you're into like, what is it, astrology?"

"Tarot. It's very different."

"Sure. But it's fate and shit?"

Esmeralda didn't feel up to the challenge of explaining why tarot was — in her opinion — very different from astrology and other divination practices.

"Kind of, I suppose."

"Last night, people kept saying that it was my destiny — my fate — to be Prez of the club."

"You don't think it is?"

"I don't believe in destiny. I don't believe in fate."

She pulled herself up, rubbed her sore head. "What do you believe in?"

He drew himself up to his fearsome full height. "I believe in me."

It was the first time Rainer had driven across the city topless. Well, to be fair, he hadn't been completely topless. He'd slipped his sleeveless club cut on, but his bare skin was still visible beneath it — his arms, his defined abs.

He attracted his fair share of wolf-whistles as his bike growled its way through the city. The whistles were mostly from women who caught sight of his muscular physique and extensive tattoos, but a couple of guys risked a whistle, too. Rainer, however, barely noticed.

His mind was racing, but he wasn't thinking about the presidency, or the club. No. All he could think about was Esme.

Last night, when she'd collapsed into him, sending his beers flying across the room, he hadn't felt angry, not even for a nanosecond. Her tight, soft body against his — the heat of her, the way she had instinctively held onto him. Seeing Esmeralda so vulnerable, so clearly distraught, had switched him straight into Daddy mode.

A mode that he didn't engage very often.

Instead of worrying about the fate of the club, and about the future of his brothers, he was thinking about why Esme had got into that state, what it was that had prompted her to drink so much, so quickly.

She was probably just after a good time. Probably forgot her limits — something that Littles do from time to time.

But he found that hard to believe. There was something so nihilistic about the way she'd been talking, about the way she'd seemed, that he couldn't help but suspect there was something more to her drunkenness than met the eye.

Then, when he'd arrived at her place, when he'd seen what a mess it was, his heart had felt even more pain for her. This morning, she'd clearly not wanted him at her place. Rainer had been hoping that when she woke, he could ask her about her life, about whether she needed

any help. Of course, that hadn't happened. It wasn't easy to broach
something like that.

But he didn't need to ask, anyway. He *knew* that she needed help.

"So, what, you think you should be the one to help her? You think
you can be her knight in shining white armor? You're such a prick,"
he muttered to himself as he pulled up onto the curb by his shop.

It was a strange feeling — this desire to defend. An unfamiliar one.
Rainer had been interested in plenty of girls before, but he'd never
felt this intense, protective feeling. Maybe it was something to do
with being nominated to be Prez of the club. Maybe it was his latent
leadership instinct coming out.

He doubted it.

He probably just had a dumb crush on Esme. He'd go for a run later,
tire himself out. That normally helped.

Rainer's shop was in a run-down industrial unit in Mott Haven,
near the South Bronx. It was one of the less picturesque parts of the
city. Around here there were mostly warehouses and factories. The
air was thick with the smell of hot plastic and oil. Still, he didn't care
about picturesque – he just wanted a space to call his own. He'd only
recently moved here from his old place in Albany, and he was pleased
to be back in the city, even if he couldn't afford anywhere a little more
central.

After much consideration, he'd decided on the name: Rainer's
Rides. He'd got a neon sign commissioned from an old friend of his
who'd studied art at the School of Visual Arts. It was a slick, bright
purple squiggle of light that was visible from half a block away.

Rainer unlocked the garage door and lifted it open. He was instantly hit with the smell of gas and grease, of leather and rust.

"Good to be home." He flipped the light switch and his current
project was illuminated, perched on a hydraulic lift so that he could

reach the underside. He was putting together something special to celebrate Baron's wedding. It was a vintage EL Knucklehead from 1936 which he'd found in pieces at a garbage dump in Florida a couple months ago. Original EL Knuckleheads were worth a small fortune — presuming that they were whole and had original parts. Something like this, though, was not too expensive. By the time it was up and running, he'd have had to replace almost half of the original bike.

No. The real cost was the days — maybe weeks — that it would take him to rebuild the whole damn hog from scratch in time for Baron's wedding.

"That's what you're good at, Rainer. Fixing up bikes. Not running a damn club." His words echoed around the surfaces of his garage. "Not saving people."

"Sage words." Rainer spun around to see who it was — he recognized the voice, but couldn't immediately place it.

Fuck. A blast from the past.

"Dog. That you?"

He'd once been the club secretary. Hard to believe that now. His hair was long and gray, scraggly and matted, pulled into a ponytail at the back of his head. Dog's cheeks were sallow and slack, and he had bristly stubble that was more white than gray.

Dog had been one of the founding members of the Drifters — a gnarled old-timer who had been a close personal friend of Marcus'. He'd fallen from grace, though. Dog had tried to push Marcus into reclaiming the club's New York territory too soon, and it had cost him dearly. After a verbal altercation with Marcus, Dog had left the club, and when he'd later tried to rejoin, he'd been banished for good.

Rainer had never exactly agreed with the banishment. He felt as though everyone deserved a second chance, no matter how badly they fucked up. Mind you, at the time, he hadn't stuck up for Dog.

"You recognized me. S'pose that's a good sign. Haven't fallen apart too much." He flashed Rainer a smile and laughed. The laugh turned into a wheezing cough.

They called him Dog because of his sharp canine teeth. Some folks said he sharpened them to make himself look fierce, but Rainer had never believed it. Dog wasn't looking so hot. He looked skinny, but no less rough than he always had. His teeth looked the same as they always had.

"Mind if I smoke?"

Rainer kind of did, but he told Dog to go ahead anyway. He got the feeling that Dog wouldn't listen to him. "Just don't come too near anything flammable."

Dog took out a cigarette, and lit the tip, being careful to stay out of the garage space.

"Been a while."

"Right," Rainer said, eying up the rear tire of the Knucklehead. It wasn't quite straight, regardless of the effort he'd put into aligning it. "Where you been?"

"Here and there. Tryna' find some other people to ride with."

"Any luck?"

"Not really. Wasn't the same. I heard about Marcus. My condolences. I know he got pissed off with me at the end, but I loved the guy."

Rainer looked at Dog. Felt like he was telling the truth.

"Thanks. Yeah. He's left a hole in our lives."

Dog took a long drag of the cigarette. "Also heard that he wanted you to be Prez."

"Well, shit. News travels fast."

Dog grinned. "Still got some friends in the club. Lots of friends, as it happens."

Well, this definitely wasn't a social call. Rainer could feel something coming, and he wasn't sure if he liked the feel of it.

"Turned it down. There's gonna be an election. I'm not the one to petition if you want to rejoin the club."

Dog shook his head. "Nope. Not my game-plan. Actually, I'm just here as a courtesy. See, I'm gonna stand in the leadership election."

Huh. Not what Rainer had been expecting. Still, it didn't bother him. The club would decide their next leader. Having people like Dog standing in the election wouldn't change that.

"Right. Well. Good luck."

Dog's eyes widened. "You don't mind?"

"Nope. The brothers will decide. Doesn't hurt to have a couple different people standing."

Another long drag of the cigarette. "So, you're not standing against me?"

"Got no plans to. Why? Should I? You got crazy ideas for the club?" Rainer was joking, but he was surprised to see Dog's face twitch as he asked.

"Not crazy ideas. I'm just gonna run the club like a damn Motorcycle Club. No more charity shit. Our members come first."

"Well, that seems reasonable." Rainer was being diplomatic, but he couldn't help but feel as though Dog was saying some troubling stuff. Charity and community engagement had always been a big part of the MCs ethos. But it wasn't his way to get involved in the running of the club.

"More than reasonable. That was why I wanted to get back into the City more quickly. I just wasn't scared of conflict like Marcus was."

Rainer felt a pang of anger — Marcus had been one of the bravest men he'd ever known. "Marcus was just more patient than you, Dog."

Dog smiled, but there was something else behind his expression.

"That's one way of looking at it." He dropped the cigarette butt and screwed it into the dirt with a boot heel. "Anyway. I'll be presenting my plan to the club. Glad to hear you're not gonna get in my way." He nodded at Rainer, then walked off.

A few moments later, Rainer heard the hum of an engine.

That pang of anger was still there, in his gut. It was growing. There was something about Dog, something about the way he'd said, "Our members come first," that had set off an alarm in Rainer.

So, without knowing exactly what he was going to do, he decided he had to act. He jumped on his bike, revved the engine, and headed in the direction of Dog's motorcycle.

The problem with streaming — or at least one of the problems — is that if you don't stick to a regular schedule, you lose viewers. Fast.

Today, Esme was doing everything she could to engage the few viewers that she had, but no-one was nibbling the bait she was putting out.

"You're telling me no-one wants a reading today? I mean sure, it's not an astronomically significant date — it's not like it's Samhain — but there must be someone who wants me to throw a few cards down."

Normally, she had a couple hundred people in her chat, pestering her to read for them, but today, there were just a few dozen. There was no chance of her getting her rent this month. None.

Oh well, that's what fate had decided.

"I believe in me." That's what Rainer had said this morning. It had been in Esme's head all day long. As bad thing after bad thing had happened to her, she'd been desperately trying to avoid taking responsibility for any of it.

But deep down, she had this annoying feeling that it was all her fault.

No, no, no, Esme, it's not your fault. Listen to destiny, float down the stream.

Finally, fate decided to smile on her when TwistOfFate43 logged on.

TwistOfFate43: *Hey gorgeous, glad to see you're online!*

"Hey Twisty, good to see you too." It made her skin crawl a little when 'random internet guys' called her gorgeous, but she couldn't complain too much. At least this guy was kind to her.

TwistOfFate43: *You OK? Seem a little low energy.*

For some reason, this question hit her hard. For a moment, she thought about shutting down the stream, and she even had to fight back tears.

Just then, another DM came through.

Come into a private chat with me. I want to make a donation. A big one.

Esme didn't think twice. She shut down the stream and opened up a private chat window.

Esme: *You there?*

TwistOfFate43: *I'm here, baby. You having a bad day?*

Esme: *Kinda. I'm fine, really.*

TwistOfFate43: *So, tell me, how much money do you need?*

Esme felt weird about this. She'd never had a chat with a fan like this before. And there was something dirty about the thought of doing it for money. She couldn't help but feel like she was using TwistOfFate43.

Esme: *Honestly, I'm OK. I don't need money.*

It felt like, for once, she was taking control of the situation. She didn't want to ask people for money, not like this. She was going to do something else.

TwistOfFate43: *I can afford it, sweetheart.*

She really didn't like to be called sweetheart by a stranger. It was making her skin crawl. Everything about this felt wrong.

Esme: *Thanks, I appreciate it, but I'm gonna say no. I'm rethinking a lot of stuff right now.*

TwistOfFate43: *Do you want me to come over?*

Esme's heart nearly jumped out of her chest when she read this message.

Esme: *Um, that's a bit scary.*

TwistOfFate43: *It's not. I can be round in like five minutes.*

Esme: *How do you know where I live?*

TwistOfFate43: *I have my ways lol.*

Esme was not laughing. This guy was five minutes away from her? And he knew where she lived? She'd been so careful about not giving away her location online. There were so many horror stories about e-stalkers and chatroom perverts. She didn't want to jump to conclusions, but this was seriously, seriously freaking her out.

TwistOfFate43: *I'll head over.*

Esme: *No. Seriously. No.*

TwistOfFate43: *Why not?*

Esme: *My boyfriend's here. He wouldn't like it.*

TwistOfFate43: *Haha, you don't have a boyfriend.*

Her heart was pounding. Maybe TwistOfFate43 was on his phone, walking toward Esme's house right now.

Esme: *Please don't come here.*

TwistOfFate43: *It would be good for us to meet. Stop being such a pricktease.*

Panicking, completely unsure what to do, Esme suddenly thought of Rainer. He'd looked after her when she'd needed it last time. She trusted him.

Without thinking about anything else, she grabbed her bag, left her computer on, and headed out to her scooter. She started the engine but was in too much of a rush to even consider wearing her helmet.

It was only after she'd been on the road for a couple of minutes that she realized that she had no idea how to get to Rainer's place. At an intersection, she felt her heart racing. It was like she was trapped in a tunnel and her anxiety was building to a ferocious peak.

She accelerated without looking, and that's when she hit something. Something hard, and big, and familiar. She shot from the scooter, skidded along the ground, and looked up into the dark New York evening. Lights coalesced into blurry smears, and she saw a concerned-looking face enter her vision.

"Rainer?" she said woozily, before the lights dimmed and went out.

CHAPTER THREE

Esme's dreams were not good. Images stuck with her: people crying, the feeling of collision, a persistent, throbbing pain in her head.

Occasionally, she'd wake up and look around, then slip back into unconsciousness before she could work out where she was.

There was a dull, ever-present sound, the beep-beep-beep of some medical machine close by. There was a smell, too. Antiseptic. Plastic. Unnatural.

Faces came and went. Some she recognized, some she didn't. All men. There was a stern-looking one she couldn't remember having seen before, and a handsome, soft-eyed guy who she was *sure* she knew, but she struggled to name.

Sleep. So much sleep. Long stretches of oblivion. And always there, in the background, a worry that next time she closed her eyes, she might never open them again.

But, luckily, she did.

And then she opened her eyes. And this time was different. She was there, all of her.

Esmeralda pulled herself up onto her elbows and coughed a couple of times. It felt as though she hadn't coughed in weeks. As she moved, she noticed that she had a tube coming out of (or going into) the inside of her elbow. It was hooked up to some kind of drip.

For a paranoid moment, she wondered whether she'd been kidnapped, drugged, and kept here against her will — wherever "here" was.

It was a dark, cozy room. Blinds were over the windows, and weak sunlight lit a far wall. There was a print on the wall: a large, beautiful, abstract painting. Was it a landscape? Was it just a few patches of color? The painting had appeared in a few of Esme's dreams, as a backdrop to the surreal goings-on her subconscious had thrown together.

"Hello?" Her voice was weak and small. As soon as she spoke, she had a dreadful thought. What if this was TwistOfFate43's place? What if he *had* come to her house and had drugged her?

Panic again. That horrible, acidic, stomach-churning rush of terror.

Esme heard the rhythm of the beeps on the machine next to her increase, getting faster and faster until, to her surprise, it let out an alarm.

There was a noise nearby, and then, a moment later, the door swung open.

To her relief, she recognized the figure.

Wearing a tight-fitting black t-shirt and thick blue jeans, it was Rainer.

"Esme? You okay?" His eyes, as soft and kind as she remembered, were full of concern.

"I... think so." She winced as her head throbbed. "My head hurts."

Rainer stepped forward. "Yeah, that's gonna happen for a while. The doctor told me."

"Doctor?"

"You don't remember?"

She shook her head.

"Fuck. You were awake. Seemed fully lucid. He was asking you questions. You don't remember any of it?"

She screwed up her face as she tried to concentrate. It was hard, like she wasn't in complete control of her brain. Thinking shouldn't be this dang hard. Eventually, a memory did float up from somewhere inside her.

"I thought that was a dream. Did he have a beard?"

"He did." Rainer was grinning. "I'm glad you remember. He said that there might be some short-term memory issues."

"What happened?"

Rainer put his hands on his hips. "Well, young lady, for the second time in two days, you bumped into me. Only this time, you happened to be riding your scooter."

It all came back. The intersection. The panic. The awful, wrong-feeling crash as she'd collided with Rainer's bike.

"I'm sorry," she said, rubbing her temple with the hand that wasn't attached to the drip. "It was all my fault."

"Well, lucky for you, I'm not going to be suing you." It was a joke, but Esme didn't really feel like laughing.

"I hate traffic. I hate driving. I hate... I'm sorry. You should sue me. I deserve it." To her surprise, tears were streaming down her cheeks.

Rainer came closer. "You mind if I get those tears for you, babygirl?" His voice was soft. Caring.

"I don't mind." She sniffed again. She could feel her nose starting to run. "I'm sorry. I don't know why I'm crying. I'm gonna get all snotty and yucky and g-g-gross." She sniffed.

"No. Nothing gross about crying." Rainer grabbed a tissue and carefully wiped it against her cheek. It was a tiny gesture, but it calmed her down. "In fact, the Doc warned me about this. He said that you would probably be more emotional and impulsive than normal for a little while, on account of your head injury. Don't worry, though, he was very clear: he didn't think there would be any lasting damage. How's your leg feeling, by the way?"

"My leg?" Now that Rainer mentioned it, she could feel some discomfort in her left shin.

"It was all bruised up. Swollen. Doc didn't think it was broken, though, and the swelling seems to have gotten better."

"How... how long have I been asleep?"

"Well, on and off, it's been about three days. You're at my place."

"All this medical equipment is yours?"

"No. The Doc's a friend of mine. Does work for Littles at a club in Brooklyn. Doesn't charge. I thought that might be best for you. But what do I know? Maybe you've got amazing insurance."

"No. No I do not."

She felt a wave of gratitude. Rainer had really considered her situation. He hadn't just bundled her into an ambulance. "If I'd known that the way to get people to be nice to me was to vomit on them, I'd have started years ago." It was a weak joke, but Rainer did her a favor and smiled anyway.

"Well, you live and learn, I guess."

Wait. Three days? That meant her rent was due. More panic.

"What's up, babygirl?"

"It's not that I'm not grateful for the way you've looked after me — I am. But... I kinda need to get going."

Rainer crossed his arms. "I'm afraid that's out of the question. Doc said that you're not going anywhere for at least another week. It's bed rest, for you."

"A week!? Bed rest?! What about yoga?!"

"Yoga?"

Esme was as surprised as Rainer that that's where her mind had gone. "It helps me. With... feelings and stuff." She didn't want to get into how important yoga was for her mental health. She was sure Rainer wouldn't understand. The thought of going a week without any yoga at all was terrifying to Esme.

"Well, we can do Little Space stuff?" suggested Rainer, to her surprise.

"Um... I dunno." She didn't know if she felt comfortable enough around him. "Sorry, I'm being such a brat. I vomit on you, smash up your bike, and you put your whole life on hold to help me." Her head was spinning.

The rent, Esme. You need to get some money.

"Look, I'll check with the Doc about the yoga. Maybe some... poses are okay?"

"Thank you," she said.

Rainer left the room, and a few moments later, she heard him on the phone.

She felt something stirring in her. A need to take control.

"I believe in me," she whispered.

"She wants to do yoga."

The voice on the other end of the phone was incredulous. "Yoga?"

"Yoga."

"She's been in a major road accident. She has a moderate to severe concussion. She is not in any kind of fit state to do yoga."

Rainer rubbed his temples. He felt dumb asking the question of Doctor Young, but at the same time, he felt completely unable to deny Esme. She wanted to do yoga, and — no matter how silly that was — he wanted to do everything he could to help her do what she wanted.

This was so crazy. He was meant to be a fucking mechanic, not a yoga facilitator. He was meant to be a badass Dom, not a coddling Daddy.

And yet...

"Maybe some of the poses, some of the less demanding ones?"

He heard a sigh on the other end of the phone. "Listen. If she can do a pose that involves her lying still on her bed and still call that yoga, then I suppose there's no harm. Maybe the breathing will do her good. But she mustn't get up yet. And when she does, you need to be there, next to her, to make sure that she doesn't fall."

He'd been tailing Dog when he'd driven into Esme. It hadn't been his fault — he'd barely had time to realize what was happening before she was skidding across the tarmac — but of course, he felt entirely responsible.

He never found out where Dog was headed, of course. Probably nowhere important. Probably just off to a liquor store knowing him.

"She seems fine so far," Rainer said, clearly distracted.

"Well, that's good. But please, follow my instructions. Bed rest for another week, and—"

But before the doctor could finish his sentence, there was a crash and a thump from the room next door — Esme's room.

Rainer didn't think. He hung up the phone and burst through the door, only to find Esme spread out across the floor. The drip bag and stand were down, and Esme had a look of agony on her face.

"Esme? What are you doing?" He crouched down next to her.

"Trying to go. I have to get out."

Rainer stroked her forehead. "You need to stay. Just for a while. You're safe here, babygirl."

"I know. But I'm not safe out there. Not safe at home."

Rainer's eyes narrowed. "What do you mean?"

"So, your landlord hasn't threatened you?"

"No." Esme was back in the bed, where she belonged for the time being. "He's been nice."

"When's your rent deadline?"

"I don't know. I can't remember. But soon."

He couldn't bear to see the pain on her face, the worry.

"Don't worry," he said. "It's all going to be okay. I'm not gonna let anything happen to you."

She nodded, but he couldn't help but feel as though there was something she was holding back. It's not like he blamed her. She probably thought he was an asshole, just like most — if not all — the Littles who were affiliated with the club did.

"You're gonna be out of here in no time."

"I'm so stupid."

It took him by surprise. "You're not."

"I am. I'm dumb. Trying to get up. I should never have done it. I need to accept my fate."

He looked at her for a moment, trying to take it all in. There was a deep wound in Esme. He could feel it. He was nowhere near getting to the bottom of it, but he knew that he wanted to.

Right now, it felt more important than just about anything else in his life.

"You're not stupid. You're not dumb."

Her pulse was getting quicker. Her face was getting paler.

"I feel funny. I think I'm going to die."

Rainer took her hand in his. "Sweetheart, listen to me, you're not going to die. You're panicking. It's normal to panic. You're not doing anything wrong."

"No-one would care if I died."

He rubbed her hand. "They would. Listen. Let's do yoga."

She snorted out a laugh.

"Not with our bodies. Just... do the breathing part. In and out. In and out."

He was so out of his depth — trying desperately to help Esme get through a panic attack by pretending to know a damn thing about yoga. But, somehow, she listened to him.

He watched as she breathed in and out, slowly. He watched as color returned to her cheeks.

"That's it, Little one," he said. "You can do this."

Then, an idea popped into his head. He got his phone out. "What's your favorite story?"

"My favorite what?"

"Story. I'm gonna read it to you."

She thought for a moment. "*James and the Giant Peach*. It was mine and my sister's favorite when we were kids."

Quick as a flash, Rainer bought and downloaded the eBook. "Right, keep holding my hand and listen."

He started to read, and as he saw her face relax, he made a decision.

CHAPTER FOUR

N O ONE HAD EVER stayed with Rainer before. It took some getting used to.

For the first couple of days, Esme stayed in bed like she was told. She wasn't too happy about it, though.

"I hate bed," became her catchphrase. She'd say it while he was bringing her dinner, she'd say it while he was helping her choose programs to watch on Netflix, she said it when he tucked her in at night.

Although she could be a little bratty at times, he loved spending time with her. Besides the fact that he could have stared into her eyes all day long if she'd let him, he found her a pleasure to talk to.

He learned about yoga — apparently, he'd been on the right track with the breathing stuff — and he learned about tarot — definitely *not* the same as astrology.

He also learned that Esme's life had been on a downward trajectory for a while. A lost job, diminishing earnings, and — by the sounds of it — a problem with taking control of just about anything. He'd decided to help her out with this month's rent.

"You can't!" she's protested. "It's not right that you should have to suffer because of how much of a shitty person I am."

"Think of it as a loan," he'd replied. "You'll pay me back when you can."

"In 2045?"

"I can wait," he chuckled.

It had been a while since he'd spent much time with anyone who wasn't completely obsessed with bikes, and it was a welcome change. It also took his mind off the messages that kept buzzing on his phone.

The texts came from different members of the Drifters. Some of them were trying to convince him to stand in the Presidential election, and some of the others were glad he *wasn't* standing. Apparently, Dog had showed up to a club meeting, and had been welcomed back into the organization by the vast majority of the members. This made sense — he still had lots of friends in the club.

Rainer — eager to show that he wasn't interested in the political runnings of the club, hadn't even bothered to attend. It made sense, really — he had to look after Esme. But, for some reason, that wasn't why he told Baron he wouldn't be attending.

"Got too much on at the garage."

He knew that if he told them that he was doting over Esme, the rumors would be hard to squash. It was, at least, partially true. He did have a lot of work to do at the garage. When he wasn't at his place with Esme, he was there, trying to put some hours into the Knucklehead restoration. He was also fixing up Esme's scooter, which was bent into a pretzel by the accident. It was a miracle that Esme hadn't been hurt worse than she had been. Silly thing hadn't even been wearing a damn helmet. Now, admittedly, Rainer didn't wear a helmet either, but — somehow — that was different.

On the second day, of Esme's stay, Doctor Young came by to check on his patient. He ran some tests, and to Rainer's relief, he seemed to think she was doing much better. He decided that it would be prudent to remove the cannula in her arm, which was just as well, since Esme had been moaning about having to drag the bag with her to the bathroom whenever she went.

"I definitely prefer food, to just... arm juice, or whatever the drip is," she said that evening, when Rainer brought her a burger for dinner. "You sure this is veggie?" she asked, holding up the limp-looking burger he'd gotten from BK.

"Positive. I checked a million times. Plus, I can tell."

"How?"

He looked at his own burger. It was, in fact, pretty much impossible to tell them apart from just looking. "A man knows real meat."

Esme snorted and copied him. "A man knows real meat." It was a squeaky approximation of his voice.

"That's what I sound like, huh?"

"That's what I sound like, huh?" she parroted, giving him a mean look before biting into her burger.

Teasing aside, he was enjoying having her stay with him.

On the third day, Esme announced that she was feeling much better.

"I know the doctor said I should stay in bed for a whole week, but that's just crazy! I'm feeling totally fine — like, back to normal. In fact, with the food you've been giving me, I kinda feel better than normal."

Try as Rainer might to get her to stay in bed, she insisted. Finally, he called Doctor Young and asked what to do.

"Look, if she's refusing to stay in bed, and you think she's of sound mind, let her get up. If she has any issues, though, let me know. And then, I think, tomorrow, if there are no more problems, she can head back to her place."

Rainer was excited but also disappointed to hear this. Life without Esme in his house would be much less colorful.

He managed to finish Esme's scooter, and he brought it back to his place on the back of an old pickup he used for jobs like this. At the end of his workday, he returned home. When he opened the front door, his eyes nearly popped out of his head.

He was staring right at Esme's perfect, peachy little ass. She was wearing the same tight black leggings she'd had on since she'd been staying with him, and she was bent over, with her hands stuck to the floor. Rainer felt an immediate rush of blood to his crotch as he watched the muscular shifting of her buttocks. Esme pushed down into her heels.

His mouth felt dry.

Fuck. Her body was incredible.

She hadn't seen him, not yet. What if she turned around and spotted him? Much to his relief, he could see that she had her earbuds in. Obviously, she hadn't heard him open the front door.

He should turn around. That's what he should do. He should turn right around and walk out, before coming back in and making a heck of a lot more noise.

Why was he still looking? Why was he still imagining what it might be like to tear those leggings open? Why couldn't he get the thought of running his tongue up and down the thin black fabric, letting her feel the warmth of his mouth against her tight pussy.

Holy fuck, this was bad. At least she hadn't seen him.

"Are you interested in yoga, Rainer?"

Oh.

"Oh, uh, hi. I didn't see you there."

She moved her feet up to her hands so that she was bending over and touching her toes. Her head appeared between her legs, looking straight at him. She even looked gorgeous upside down.

"Didn't see me, huh?"

"Right. I just... thought you were part of the couch." He pointed over at a piece of furniture that looked absolutely nothing like a person.

"I get mistaken for a couch a lot," she said, slowly rising up, putting her hands above her head.

Rainer couldn't help but notice that as she stood on her tiptoes, her butt shifted a little and her ass cheeks made the most delicious shape.

Spank her, Rainer. Just head over there and spank her. She's asking for it.

"Well, I'm glad that you're feeling well enough to do some yoga."

"Yeah!" she turned round, grinned at him. "It always makes me feel better."

"What's so good about yoga? It's just like a mild workout, right?"

Esme shook her head in disbelief. "It's so much more than a workout, Rainer. It's like... the way you get your body and soul to talk to each other."

"Sounds interesting." He dumped down a bag of tools he'd brought back from his shop. "Good news. Your scooter is pretty much fixed. And I spoke to the doctor. He said that you can head off tomorrow. Clean bill of health."

Rainer was sad that her stay with him was going to come to a premature end, but he couldn't keep her here forever, regardless of whether he wanted to.

She grinned, then her smile dropped. "You know, I was kinda getting used to being around you."

"Me too," he admitted. "But, you know, it's not like we never have to see each other again."

"Right."

"We could go for a drink."

"As friends?"

"Sure." He could feel the tension rising. He tried with all his might to keep his eyes on her face, not let them glance down at her ample breasts, squeezed together beneath her low-cut vest top. "Two friends."

"Say, I had an idea."

"Oh yeah?"

"I need to pay you back. For the loan for my rent, and because you fixed up my scooter."

He raised his hands. "Whenever you can. There's no rush."

"I just thought of a way I could pay you back a little bit. Something a little..." she licked her lips, "unconventional." There was a flash of mischief in her eyes. He couldn't help but think about what those soft, pink lips might look like wrapped around the shaft of his cock.

That's not what she meant though, obviously.

Was it?

"Sure. What did you have in mind?"

Another flash of mischief. "Follow me."

The deep, earthy scent of sage and sandalwood. Dim candlelight. The glow of warmth and intimacy.

Preparing the space had been a quick job, but Esme was relatively pleased with the results.

"How did you get rid of the stink of oil? It smells magical in here." Rainer looked half-confused, half-amused.

"Glad to hear it. It might seem silly but putting yourself in an altered mental state can be as simple as smelling something unusual and seeing a familiar place in a new context."

"Wait a second, where did you get all this stuff? You weren't meant to leave the house." Rainer looked at her with an accusatory expression.

"Um... I just... found all this stuff... somewhere. In a cupboard." She knew that she looked as guilty as sin, but it didn't feel as though Rainer was *really* annoyed with her. "A cupboard that you haven't opened for years."

Of course, Esme had left the house. You didn't just find sage and sandalwood growing on trees. She'd actually been very obedient while she'd been staying at Rainer's place. It had only felt right. Rainer had been so kind and caring during her stay, that she wanted to repay him with respect.

Only problem was, she'd also wanted to surprise him with this tarot reading. So that meant sneaking out while he was at work. Esme had been pretty sure that he'd be alright with it, though. He was more understanding and easy-going than she'd first thought.

It had been a real treat to have someone feeding her and looking after her for a couple days, a nice vacation from the reality of her — admittedly limited — responsibilities. Plus, there was that thrill, the thrill of getting to know someone new. Someone... interesting.

The only thing that had surprised her was that she hadn't told him about the situation with TwistOfFate43. She didn't want him worrying about it. Plus, the more she thought about it, the more she convinced herself that it was just some wacko who didn't *really* know where she lived. She'd just block him on Twitch and get back to a normal life.

Rainer chuckled. "Ah yes. My forgotten, sacred, ritual cupboard. Of course that's where you found all this."

Esme had prepared a small ritual area for him. Esme looked at her handiwork — an incense burner, and some deep, dark fabrics thrown across the bed. She'd lain out a simple tarot mat, and she had a deck laid out next to it.

Rainer kept his house pretty neat and tidy, but that was quite easy when he didn't spend much time here. From what Esme had picked up, he spent the majority of his waking hours at his garage. This was just a place to sleep and, sometimes, eat.

His bedroom had had no real personality. Now that it was decked out like a new-age shrine, it had plenty.

"Come take a seat, pilgrim," she said, gesturing toward the bed.

You're about to go to bed with Rainer Ortiz.

"You're not gonna cast some kinda funky spell on me, are you?"

"Of course I am. You're going to be obeying my every whim by the end of the session."

"Sounds pretty fucking kinky."

Okay, well now Esme's heart was pounding like a drum. He had to know what kind of a reaction a sentence like that would elicit from her, right? He had to know how deeply she was crushing on him, how hard she'd been crushing on him for months.

"Take a seat," was all that she could say, trying desperately to stop her cheeks from burning, hoping that he wouldn't stare at her cheeks too hard.

Like the way he was staring at your other cheeks a couple minutes ago.

They sat opposite each other on the bed, with the tarot mat between them. It was a nice, big bed, plenty of space for two people. And obviously, Esme's brain went *there* again.

"So, what's the point of this, exactly?" Rainer asked. There was something infuriatingly sexy about his obvious cynicism. She was determined to show him that this wasn't all just some kooky nonsense.

"It can have all sorts of points," she said, shuffling the cards carefully. "It depends what you're trying to get out of it. Some people believe that a higher power — something like God, or angels, or fate — controls which cards come up. Some people don't. Some people believe that the cards themselves are trying to tell you something. Some people believe that the answers are all inside you, and that the cards are just a tool to facilitate self-realization."

"So... what do you think?"

"Fate." It was a simple word, but it hung between them for a moment. The silence that followed was thick and complete.

You bumped into him in the club. You bumped into him on his bike. Now you want to bump into him in another way...

"Fate is bullshit."

"You're entitled to think that, but I think you'll find that the cards have something else to say." She finished shuffling the cards and placed the deck to the right of the mat. "Most people come to the deck with a question. Do you have anything you want to ask?"

Rainer was silent for a moment, then he folded his arms. "You know, seeing as I'm doing this, I might as well ask an actual question that's on my mind. Fuck it."

"Yeah, throw yourself into it. What have you got to lose?"

"Right. So. Dear tarot cards: should I stand for election to be President of the Drifters?"

Esme was taken aback. While she'd been staying with Rainer, he'd said a couple of times that he had no interest in running the club. Maybe he wasn't quite as certain as he'd implied.

"Good question, but it's best to avoid yes/no questions. Maybe you could rephrase it?"

"Hmm, okay. What about this: what are my real feelings about being the President of the Drifters?"

"Perfect. This way there's plenty of room for us to feel out the answer together."

"Yeah, I got the sense that it wasn't gonna be as simple as yes or no."

"I'd like you to focus on the question at as deep a level as you can. Think it through. It's not just about the idea of leading the club. It's about so much more than that. It's about who you are, right?"

"Right. Fine. I'll do my best to think about it." He did seem to be thinking. Concentrating. She could feel a shift in the energy of the room. Like a connection was forming between her and Rainer. Something deep. Something real.

"We're gonna do a past, present, future reading. Ready?"

"Ready," he breathed back, gave her a look so intense it made her pussy do a backflip.

As she turned over the first card, she could feel the tension building. Rainer, too, looked as though he could feel it.

Card one. The past. The King of Swords.

Rainer reacted with interest. "What does that mean? I'm gonna fight someone?"

"By themselves, the cards don't mean anything. It's about how they relate to each other. This — the past — could imply Marcus. He could be the King of Swords. The card often depicts a harsh but fair commander. Someone decisive."

"That sounds like Marcus. His word was law."

"Marcus did a fantastic job leading the Drifters, all the way 'til the end."

"Right."

Card two. The present. The Five of Pentacles.

"This card is to do with paranoia. About a lack of trust."

Rainer was suddenly extremely focused. "Trust?"

"Do you struggle with trust, Rainer?"

He didn't answer, but he looked extremely disturbed.

"There's something about anger, too. Sometimes, the King of Swords can be overly authoritarian. Maybe that card doesn't refer to Marcus. Someone else in your past? Someone stopping you from feeling trust? Does that sound right?"

Rainer's face paled. He looked white as a sheet. "How the hell do you know that?" Esme was surprised by how angry he sounded.

"I don't," she said, backtracking. "It's just the card."

"Finish the damn reading," he grunted.

She wasn't scared, exactly, but she felt suddenly very uncomfortable. As she reached for the final card, she wondered if she'd made a terrible mistake doing this with Rainer.

Card three. The future: The Nine of Pentacles.

Damn. It had to be that card. She already knew that Rainer wasn't going to like this.

"You have to deal with your trust issues. The only way to get to a positive outcome is by confronting whatever happened to you and moving forward."

Rainer didn't reply.

"Someone hurt you, didn't they?" Esme reached out to him, but when she touched his hand, he flinched.

"I think you'd better leave." His voice was calm but completely detached.

"Leave?"

"Right now."

"I'm sorry, I ju—"

With a roar, Rainer stood. "I said *right now*."

Esme felt a pang of fear, and deep, deep sadness. But worst of all, she hadn't told him the full reading: there was no easy way out. There was deep hardship ahead for Rainer, and she couldn't help but feel as though she was bound up in it.

Because the Nine of Pentacles was her birth card.

CHAPTER FIVE

P EOPLE SAY ANGER IS a wave. Or that it's an explosion.

But for Rainer, that wasn't the case. For Rainer, anger was a tide. Once it came in, he had a long, long wait ahead of him before it went out again.

It was still with him the next morning. Of course, he wasn't angry with Esme — far from it. He was furious with himself. He'd gotten very good at being angry with himself over the years. It was easy as slipping on a pair of comfy shoes.

The anger was still with him after he rode to his garage. It was still with him as he worked all day long on Baron's hog, and it still didn't leave him when he decided to head to the Den after he finished work.

He was, of course, partly hoping that he'd see Esme at the bar. It was unlikely. He'd obviously scared her. He doubted that she ever wanted to see him again. She'd probably avoid anywhere he went regularly like the plague.

Why had he done it? Why had he let his past take control of him like that?

Esme hadn't done anything wrong. All she'd done was interpret a fucking piece of card, and she'd done it so broadly that basically every single person on the planet would have seen something of themselves in the reading.

But it had felt as though what she'd said was designed to get under his skin. It felt so *specific* to him and his history. He hated to think back to that dark time in his life, a time when it felt as though he *was* fated for something awful. A time when — through no fault of his own — he'd ended up derided and hated by society.

As he pushed open the door to the Den, he did what he always did — stuffed the memory so far down into his subconscious that he wouldn't have to deal with it again for a while.

At least now there was no question of anything romantic happening with Esme. He could forget about the presidential contest and get on with just being a mechanic.

"You look like someone shat in your beer."

God damn you, Baron, and your observations.

"I'm fine."

Wolf shook his head. "No way. I can tell you're fucked off because of your lip."

"He's so right," Baron said, prodding a finger into Rainer's chest. "When you're angry, your lower lip quivers."

Rainer very pointedly bit his lip. "You know, I came here to avoid my problems, not engage with them."

"Well, we *are* your problems, brother." Wolf grinned.

"Tell me about it," Rainer replied.

"No, tell *me* about it," Baron quipped.

Rainer sighed.

"You know, I kind of assumed we'd be talking about the future of the club, not of your love life." Baron raised a drink to his lips.

The sound of classic rock pumped out of the jukebox. Crank was in here tonight, with a couple old drinking buddies from an affiliated

MC. They kept pumping out cheesy hits. Guns N' Roses, Led Zeppelin, and Pink Floyd.

It was a strange soundtrack to the discussion, although Rainer couldn't think of any particular tracks which would make this conversation any less awkward.

"Might be one and the same if Rainer pulls his finger out and runs for the presidency."

"Can we please just focus on Esme? I'm not running for Prez. I'm not the right person, and that's that."

"Well, the situation with Esme is easy. Clearly, she needs the help of a Daddy." Baron looked at Rainer pointedly.

"You think?"

"She's lost her way. I mean, she's always had her head in the clouds, but right now, she's floating so high, I doubt there's any air up there for her to breathe at all."

"Even if she *does* need a Daddy, I'm not the right person," Rainer said. "I scared her."

"So apologize." Wolf spoke as though it was the easiest thing in the world.

"I told her to leave my fucking house. For no reason."

"Well, make it a really fucking good apology, then."

Rainer always struggled to take advice. Even when he knew the advice was good. He'd known Wolf and Baron for years, but he didn't really know if he could say that he *trusted* them. It was his problem, not theirs.

"I don't know."

There was a howl of excitement as the intro to "Here I Go Again" by Whitesnake thundered out from the bar's speakers.

"Fuck, I thought I took this tune off the list," Wolf said.

"You look a bit like a silver-haired David Coverdale," Baron joked.

"You're barred."

"You know what I think I should do?" Rainer said.

The chorus sounded out: "Here I go again on my own!"

"What's that?" Baron replied.

"What I always do. Listen to my own advice."

He finished his drink and headed for the door. Halfway there, he glanced down. There was a stain on the carpet. It was right here that she'd bumped into him. Hard to tell if the stain was drink or vomit.

I believe in me.

Esme could feel the sweat on her brow. Dang. Why was this so hard? This position was never normally this difficult. Clearly, her normal strength and stamina was still a little way off.

"Remember, honey, keep those arms in, straight in line."

Kelly's voice was always soothing, even when she was correcting Esme's form.

In response, Esme let out a little grunt of effort and tried to tuck her elbows in, just like she knew she should. There was a trembly burn in her core as she did her best to maintain a steady plank.

"That's it," Kelly said. "You're doing great, my little warrior."

It was convenient that Esme's best friend also happened to be her yoga instructor. Kelly Hampton was a dream. Tall, slim, lithe, and supple as a willow branch. She had sparkly blue eyes and the cutest dimples in existence. Esme had been in awe of her ever since the two of them had met at a hot yoga center in Manhattan three years ago.

After the session, they'd decided to grab a coffee together. The chemistry between them had been instant. Making stupid faces, doing dumb impressions of the know-it-all yoga instructor, taking long sniffs of each other's coffee and pretending to be able to smell all kinds of unusual scents. Turned out that as well as being fun and naughty, Kelly was insanely ambitious and clearly interested in learning and bettering herself. In short, she was everything that Esme aspired to be but probably never would.

At the time, Esme had been faintly dumbstruck that someone like Kelly would have wanted to spend time with her. She kept waiting for the moment that Kelly revealed that she didn't really want to be her friend, and that it was all some sick prank. But the moment never came.

A coffee became two coffees, and then two coffees became a very long and chuckle-full afternoon drink. By the end of the evening, they'd both made a solemn promise to each other: they'd be qualified yoga instructors within the year.

Kelly, of course, had done it.

But here they were, three years later, and Esme was nowhere near her goal.

She moved through her *vinyasa* one more time, transitioning from plank to up-dog, then shifting her weight back into a downward-facing dog, poking her butt as high up into the sky as she could.

Her heart wasn't in it, and — like the excellent instructor she was — Kelly picked up on it.

"You okay, Esme? Still tired from the accident?"

"Uh-huh," Esme replied miserably. "It's like my body doesn't want to play ball."

"Want a break?"

Kelly had agreed to help Esme with practice for her teaching course. Trouble is, no amount of training and learning would ever solve Esme's problem. She already knew *how* to teach yoga. The fact was, even if she was the most technically proficient, gifted practitioner of yoga on the planet, she knew she'd never be able to stand up in front of a group of people and actually teach them.

She was too dang scared.

"I think that's me done for the day." Esme collapsed onto the mat, letting her cheek smoosh down. "Time for a forty-eight-hour long *shavasana*." She rolled over onto her back, then spread her arms and legs out into the classic corpse-pose shape. Instructors often said that *shavasana* was the most important pose in yoga.

That suited Esme, because there was nothing she liked more than to lie on her back and let her worries drift away into the ether.

As she looked up, she thought about how beautiful this yoga studio was. It was a stark contrast to the space she practiced yoga in her own home. Obviously, Kelly had built this entire space herself. As well as being an accomplished yoga instructor, she just so happened to be a carpenter. She ran a bunch of public classes from a studio downtown, but she also did one-on-one tuition in her home studio.

Everything was neat and tidy. Kelly had built a shelf for offerings. Today, Esme had put the cards she'd pulled for Rainer on the shelf, to try to think about what it was that had upset him so much. She'd tried to keep the reading in her mind as she moved through the yoga sequence, but she'd been too distracted by her body's weakness to reach any conclusions.

"Come on, sugar, let's talk it through."

"Talk what through?" Esme said, closing her eyes.

"Whatever's bothering you." Kelly walked over to the offering shelf. "Or rather — whoever it was that you pulled these cards for."

"He asked you to leave?"

Esme nodded, deeply inhaling the scent of her chamomile tea. "It was like I'd touched a nerve, and he just snapped."

"Didn't give you any clues about why?"

"Nope."

Rain drummed against Kelly's huge kitchen window. Esme tracked the streaks as they flowed down the glass.

"Have you heard from him since? Any apology?"

"Not a thing. It was only yesterday, but I admit, I'd been hoping that he might get in touch. It's annoying, because last night I wanted to spend some time in Little Space, just relax in front of some cartoons with Om Baby, but I couldn't. I was so worried about him and about what had happened that I felt sick to my stomach."

"Poor girl," Kelly said, stroking Esme's arm.

Kelly wasn't a Little, but she'd never been anything but supportive about Esme's lifestyle.

"It's okay. I just... I kinda thought he liked me."

"Yeah. That sucks. I get the feeling you wanted to see if he might be your Daddy."

"It's weird. I always thought he hated me before. Maybe it's because I think everyone hates me."

"No one could hate you, dumb-dumb. You're lovely." Kelly rested her head against her arm.

"They're all judging me, though. Watching me and laughing."

"It's holding you back from teaching, huh? That feeling."

Esme nodded. She knew where the feeling came from. She could pinpoint the exact moment that she started to feel scared of people. It was the same moment that she lost the ability to take control of her whole life. The same moment she just decided to submit to fate.

"Wish I could make it go away."

"You know, it sounds like Rainer's been through some stuff." Esme could tell from the way Kelly said it that she was also saying: "Just like *you've* been through some stuff."

"Probably."

"He probably was just freaked out. Like there was a memory he didn't want to relive."

"I can relate to that."

"Right. I'm not saying you should just forgive him, exactly. I dunno. It's more like, maybe he just deserves a second chance. Or a chance to explain."

Esme pouted. "Yeah well, if he shows up at my front door, ready to apologize, I guess I'll hear him out." Then, under her breath, she added, "But that's never gonna happen."

It was an old photo album, bound in something that looked and felt like leather, but probably wasn't. Esme sat on her couch, with her legs crossed, surrounded by clothes and discarded scraps of paper. Om Baby was perched on the edge of the table, eyes closed, arms in eagle pose.

Reliving memories. For most people it was a pleasure. For Esme, though, it was like an endurance challenge.

She flipped the album open. On the first page were her baby photos. Next to them were dates and labels in her mom's looping handwriting.

Esme having dinner. Esme smiling. Esme being a silly onion.

She had been a smiley baby, but the smiles got even bigger after her sister was born.

There were pictures of Esme, aged four, with her sister on her lap. Esme had this grin on her face, like she was the luckiest, happiest person on the planet. She looked at pictures of her and her sister in the bathtub, surrounded by bubbles. There was a shot of the two of them at a zoo. Esme's sister was pointing at a massive pile of elephant poop.

Esme snorted with laughter. She swore that she had an actual memory of that day, even though she'd only been five or six.

She turned the page.

There was her sister, as she remembered her. School uniform on. Hair in pigtails. Sabrina Adams.

Esme felt a horrible feeling in her stomach. The pain and sadness started to bubble up, and quickly threatened to overwhelm her.

That's the exact moment that she heard a knock at the front door.

Instantly, her thoughts went back to what she'd said to Kelly just a couple hours ago. *If he shows up at my front door, ready to apologize...*

She felt a surge of hope, and pushed the photo album shut, then she grabbed Om Baby, before running to the front door.

But when she pushed it open, it wasn't Rainer staring back at her.

Not even close.

CHAPTER SIX

"Esme?"

The man in her doorway was in his early thirties, with small, fast-blinking eyes and a mouth that was fixed in a smile that looked as though it was taking a little too much effort to be genuine. His lank hair came down past his ears.

"Do I know you?"

"You do! You really do!"

The man clasped his hands together. He was wearing a drab, taupe hoody, which hung off his skinny body. He looked kind of like a non-threatening, beige ghost.

"Umm, sorry I don't recognize you."

"I bet you'll work it out in a minute." He pulled a long curtain of hair away from his face. It wasn't helping Esme, though. "Think about it, Esme. Who's you're biggest fan? Who would come all the way across the country to make sure that you had plenty of money for this month's rent?" The man reached his hand into his pocket and pulled out an untidy stack of twenty-dollar bills, before brandishing them at her.

As Esme realized who it was, she felt a horrendous icy feeling in her gut. It suddenly felt as though all the color was being drained from her vision, and the world slowed down to a crawl.

"Twist of fate?"

The man smiled, more freely this time. As his lips parted, she saw that his teeth were cracked and yellowed. "It's me! Your savior."

She felt an instant urge to run, to kick him in the balls and run as far and as fast away from here as she possibly could.

Why hadn't she told Rainer about this guy? He'd never have let her leave his place if he'd known that there was a stalker on the loose. And why had she managed to convince herself that he didn't actually know her address? This was insanity. She was going to die.

"Um... I don't know how I feel about this." She didn't want to enrage him, or make him think she was angry or ungrateful for him being here. She had to keep him distracted until she could think of a plan.

"I get it, I get it! This is weird, deeply weird. You're probably like: 'Oh no! A stalker's here to kill me'!" He let out a weak laugh. "Eek! A psychopath knows where I live!"

Esme mirrored his laugh. "It's a bit random, yeah."

Stay calm, Esme. Don't do anything rash. You don't know what this guy is capable of.

"Haha, I know, right? But don't worry, I'm not here to kill you. Damn, can I just say, you're even more beautiful in real life than you are on stream?"

"Right."

"Fuck. I'm getting this all wrong. I'm probably coming across as a creep, aren't I?"

Esme didn't know how to answer this. She decided that the safest option was to try not to upset this guy. "No way. You're just nervous, right?"

"You're so understanding! I knew you'd appreciate me being here."

For the first time in her life, Esme wished that she had a panic button. If there was some way she could have had the police on call right now, she would have done it in an instant.

"So, are you gonna invite me in? I've come a long way."

She remembered him saying in the private chat that he was only five minutes away, but she wasn't about to bring that up now. "Where have you come from?"

Twist of Fate was about to answer, but he stopped himself before holding up a finger and waggling it at Esme.

"Clever. Very clever. Trying to get my address out of me, right? So you can find out who I am?"

"N-no! I just... I was just trying to have a conversation."

"Don't bullshit me, Esmeralda. I know you." There was a nasty tone in his voice. "You're scared. You don't need to be scared. I'm a nice guy."

Esme's fear and panic was rising fast. Her heart was pounding, and it almost felt as though she was outside her own body, watching this situation unfold. All of a sudden, she felt an overwhelming urge to act. She had to do something, and she had to do it right now.

Without doing anything that would betray what she was about to do, Esme grabbed the front door, and slammed it tightly shut.

Or at least, she would have done, if Twist of Fate hadn't stuck his foot in the way.

Esme tried to heave the door into its frame, but she was still weak. Twist of Fate was stronger than he looked.

"Esme! Don't make this weird!" he grunted, pushing the door open.

"What do you want?" she sobbed, shrinking back from him. Om Baby was on the table, watching her, willing her to be okay.

"I just want to be near you," said her intruder. "I just want a tarot reading. I brought money."

"This isn't right," she said. "I'm scared."

"You don't need to be scared," he said. Then he took out something from his other pocket. It gleamed in the light — a pair of solid metal handcuffs.

"What's that for?" Esme asked.

"You don't have to be scared. I just have to make sure you don't run, that's all. I've come all this way just to see you. To hear you read my tarot in person. I'm not having you run. Not this time."

There was something particularly chilling about the way he said, "Not this time." What did he mean?

"Don't put them on me," Esme said, her voice quiet, barely even there. "Please, I don't want this. This isn't right."

"It's for your own good. I'm gonna pay you for your time. I'll pay you for anything that you want to give me."

Esme felt the tears as she realized that she was powerless. Once again, she was transported back to that place: a place of fear and shame, a place of deep, deep hurt.

Then, she felt the cold metal close around her wrist.

Twist of Fate tugged her gently, moving her into her own home, as he searched for a place to lock her. And just before he clasped the other side of the handcuff to a table leg, there was a gruff, furious voice from the doorway.

"Take your fucking hands off her this instant."

It was Rainer. He was here.

The rat of a man who'd put a handcuff around Esme's wrist froze. He turned to look at Rainer, a nervous, shit-eating grin on his face.

"Chill dude," he said, before he had a chance to take Rainer in. The guy's eyes scanned up and down Rainer's impressive, imposing form. He took in the frayed denim cut — the MC badge stitched over the biker's heart. No doubt he clocked the tattoos inked over bulging arms as Rainer stood with his hands on his hips. "J-just chill."

"I don't chill," Rainer said, pounding a pounding his right fist into his left palm. "I really don't fucking chill, shit-stain."

"It's not what it looks like," the shit-stain stammered. "It's all consensual, my dude. Just a bit of slap and tickle."

"So, what does it look like?" Rainer asked, taking another step forward. He was sure that this scumbag wasn't here on Esme's invitation. He'd never been gladder to follow his gut. He'd been close to not coming, really fucking close.

If it hadn't been for that damn stain on the carpet, he'd probably be at his shop right now, cluelessly working on Baron's hog. And Esme would be here, alone, having to deal with... this. The thought made him feel sick.

"I d-don't know."

"He wasn't listening to me," Esme said, her voice trembling. "I asked him to leave."

"That true?" Rainer asked.

The shit-stain held up his hands. "No. I mean, I was just leaving. I was just here to give Esme a—"

"Don't you dare say her fucking name!" Rainer bellowed, surprising himself with his anger. "I don't ever want to hear her name out of your lips again! You understand? You're not worthy of breathing the same fucking air as her, let alone saying her name."

Shit-stain flinched. "I get it, I get it, I won't say her name. I was just here to give her this money." He pointed to a pile of cash on the carpet.

"I don't want his money," Esme said.

"In that case, I figure there's no good reason for you being here."

"I'll go! I'll go!"

Rainer thought about this for a second. He'd found this guy alone with Esme, clearly making her act against his will. There was no way that he was letting him leave.

"I don't think so," Rainer said.

"You c-can't keep me here."

Then, before he waited for Rainer to reply, Shit-stain bolted for the door. But Rainer was quicker. As the guy shot past him, Rainer turned, grabbed at his arm, and gripped his wrist tight.

"Let me go."

"No can do."

Esme sniffed. "Just let him go, Rainer. He's not worth your trouble."

"Sorry, darling," Rainer said, "Not happening." Then, while he held onto the guy's arm, he pulled out his phone and dialed 911.

The cops, sadly, were useless. They took the guy away but told Rainer and Esme that there was little that they could do in this instance. There was no evidence that the guy had broken in, and — because Rainer had removed Esme's handcuff with a screwdriver — no evidence that he'd tried to hold her against her will.

The biggest insult had come when the lead cop — a thick-set guy with a terrible handlebar mustache — had asked him about his MC.

"You a one-percenter? Should I be running your name through the computer?"

Rainer did not want his criminal record to be under consideration.

"With respect, sir, I decline to answer that question."

Esme had looked a little confused. Still, better that she was confused than she found out that he'd done time in prison for fucking drug dealing.

It was a bust, overall, but Rainer hoped that he'd put the fear of God into the little shit-stain. He had to be less likely to do something like this again, and that was the main thing.

After the cops were gone, Esme was still, understandably, freaking out.

"You gonna tell me what that was all about, sweetheart?"

"Maybe. You gonna tell me why you called the cops when I asked you to let him go?"

"Gladly." Rainer rubbed his forehead. "Shall we head somewhere else though? No offense, but this place is a damn pigsty."

"It's homely."

"Homely to pigs."

Esme, luckily, smiled at this. "Fine. Let's go somewhere."

At a bar round the corner, the two of them sat at a table as electronic dance music thrummed in the background.

"He was a fan of yours?"

"I guess."

Rainer had a sudden thought. "So, the streaming you do, is it like... Onlyfans? No judgment from me, you understand."

"It's not like that. Although I've thought about doing that. It's just tarot reading."

"Right. You said that you used to do that at a store."

"Yeah, and now I do it online."

Rainer sighed. "I owe you an apology. No. Fuck. I owe you two apologies."

"You cuss a lot."

"I do. I should tone it down. You want me to tone it down?"

"Don't care."

She obviously *did* care. "I'll tone it down. Number one apology: I'm sorry that I got angry and asked you to leave the other day. It was unacceptable. You didn't do a fu— a *single* thing wrong." He managed to stop himself before he cussed again.

"Apology accepted. I know that sometimes tarot readings can stir some powerful feelings. There's nothing wrong with getting angry."

"Yeah, but I shouldn't express it like a dam—" he stopped himself again. "Like a child. Apology number two: I should have explained why I was gonna call the cops before doing it. I'm sorry."

"But you're not sorry for calling the cops?"

"Nope. Had to do it."

"Why?"

He took a long sip of his drink.

Fuck it. Here goes nothing.

"Esmeralda, I care about you. I don't know how long I've felt like this. Feels like it's always been this way."

Her eyes widened. "You... care about me?"

"Mmmhmm. I know I've always seemed gruff. You probably think I'm an asshole. I mean, um, an A-hole. I've never been good at relationships. Not just romantic ones. Not that this *is* romantic." He was struggling here. He'd never been good at expressing himself. Still, he kept going. "And not that it isn't romantic. Not that this is even a relationship. Ugh. All I mean is, I'm going to look after you. You need someone to take care of you. To stick up for you. To believe in you. I can feel it. Ever since we bumped into each other at the Den, my Daddy side has been going wild." Without realizing, he reached out and took hold of her hand, gently stroking the top of her knuckles.

"I called the cops," he continued, "because I didn't have a choice. My Daddy side was screaming at me that I had to do it for your safety, whether you felt it was the right thing to do in that moment or not. Let me ask you a question. Are you a fan of confrontation?"

"No," she admitted.

"How do you feel about upsetting people?"

"Hate it more than just about anything else in the world."

"That's what I figured," he smiled. "So of course you didn't want to call the cops. You just wanted to see the back of that guy and hope that you'd never see him again, right?"

She nodded.

"Normally, I'd have beaten the cr...ud out of him. But I didn't want to do that because then *he* could have had *me* arrested, and I don't want to be apart from you." It was like he'd turned on a faucet. Now that he'd started talking, he just couldn't stop. "I want to help you, babygirl. If you want me to. I want to help you with your issues. I want to help you with your self-esteem, with your money problems. I can see a beautiful, shining gem inside you, and I want to help the rest of the world to see just how perfect that gem is."

For a moment, for a perfect, silent moment, she just stared into his eyes. She was so beautiful — so insanely, unattainably perfect. He was crazy to think that she'd ever agree to something like this.

"A-are you asking if I want you to be my Daddy?"

His heart pounded in his chest.

I believe in me.

Time to be bold.

"That's exactly what I'm asking. It'll be your choice. And if we do it, then we'll do it properly. Contracts, documents, safewords, whatever you want."

She bit her lip. Her perfect, kissable lip.

"Take your time to think about it. I know you're vulnerable right now. You don't need to rush into an—"

"Yes," she said. "The answer's yes."

So much relief. "Good. Then I'm not going to let you out of my sight. Which could prove a *little* tricky."

CHAPTER SEVEN

T HAT NIGHT, AFTER COOKING a healthy dinner of pasta and
vegetables, Rainer spent a little time tidying up Esme's place
before it was her bedtime.

"Don't get used to this," he said, picking up all the clean clothes that
were strewn around the small apartment. "I'm just getting you started.
From tomorrow, you're gonna have a clean-up routine, which you'll
stick to religiously."

"I don't think I've ever stuck to anything religiously," Esme said
absentmindedly.

"Now's the time to start," Rainer said, organizing her whites and
her coloreds into separate piles.

"When are we going to do all the contracty stuff?"

Rainer felt as though it was a good sign that Esme hadn't been
worrying too much about the business with the stalker from earlier
in the day. Hopefully Shit-stain was still at some cold, boring police
station, being interviewed about what had happened that day.

"Tomorrow evening, I think," he replied.

"Why not tonight?" she whined. "I can't wait."

"Because I need to organize it. Plus, tomorrow, during the day,
there's a meeting that we kind of have to go to."

"Uggggghhhh," she groaned. "I hate meetings."

"Well, this one's important."

Rainer hadn't been planning to go to this particular meeting, but something had changed in him since he opened up to Esme about his feelings for her. Something fierce and protective and all-encompassing.

"Booooorriiinnngggg." The word seemed to last forever.

"Oh hello," Rainer said, spotting a cute little stuffie sitting on the edge of a table. It looked kind of like a bunny rabbit, but it had longer than normal arms and legs. "What's your name?"

"That's Om Baby," Esme said. "She's annoyingly good at yoga, and she never gets freaked out or worried about anything."

"Pleased to meet you, Om Baby," Rainer said. "Are *you* gonna come to the meeting tomorrow, too? I'd like you to."

"Om Baby says, '*Namaste*.' And she also says that she'll think about coming to the meeting. But she only really wants to go if she can go in your pocket."

"Sounds perfect," Rainer said.

Hopefully, everyone else would be fine with Rainer bringing along Esme and Om Baby. Although something told him that it might raise a couple of eyebrows.

The rest of the evening was blissful. Rainer waited while Esme had a shower, then he watched her brush her teeth. After that, he read her a bedtime story, and soon, she was ready for sleep.

"You know," she said, yawning, "I don't remember the last time I was in bed by this time. I also can't remember the last time I did a whole bedtime routine. It feels... magic."

"You are magic," Rainer said. Then he leaned over, and gently kissed her forehead.

"You enjoyed that, didn't you?"

Rainer looked back at Esme as she took her helmet off. There was a huge, unstoppable grin on her face.

"That was so much better than riding a scooter. I *totally* get bikes now."

"Yeah, it's about a billion times more fun than a scooter."

They hopped off, and Rainer chained his hog next to the twenty or so other motorbikes which were fastened near the entrance of the Den.

"You ready, sweetheart?"

Esme paused for a moment. "I like it when you call me that."

"Good."

"I really like it, Daddy."

He felt a hum in his chest. Fuck. He could get used to that.

"Is Om Baby safe?" Esme asked.

Rainer checked his pocket. Thankfully, the blissed-out little stuffie was safely stowed away in there.

"You know, I—" Rainer was interrupted by a hard slap on the back, followed by a firm squeeze on his shoulder.

"Glad you listened to our advice." It was Baron, looking almost as happy as Esme.

"I didn't," Rainer replied. "I just listened to my heart."

"Hi, Baron," Esme said.

"You here for the meeting, too?"

"Uh-huh."

The grizzled blacksmith raised an eyebrow. "Not sure how well that's gonna go down with Dog's contingent."

"Yeah, well they're just gonna have to f…" he glanced at Esme, "*frogging* deal with it."

"Frogging good save," Esme said.

"Hey, no cussing," Rainer joked.

"What?!"

"He's right," Baron joined in. "To a toad, that's about as bad of a word as you can say."

"Tradition." The word rang out across The Den like a gunshot. "It's what Marcus stood for. And it's what I'll bring back to The Drifters."

Dog was in the middle of what was basically a speech pitching himself as the President of the club. In a way, it didn't matter what he said, because he was still the only person standing to be Prez. He could have said that they'd be focusing exclusively on petting cats, and he'd still have been elected.

He was wearing his cut — the item of clothing that he'd publicly removed about a year ago as he'd left the club. It was adorned with a brand-new patch, but it clearly still hadn't been cleaned. That was one of the unbreakable rules of the club — you don't clean your cut, no matter what.

"In the past few years, we've gone soft." Dog walked back and forth at the front of the bar, his thick boots striking the ground hard with each step. "I get it. We've got big hearts. We ain't criminals like some of the other bastard clubs that run in this state." He snorted, then spat down onto the ground.

"Trouble is," Dog continued, "If we don't fight fire with fire, then we're gonna be in serious trouble. Other clubs are gonna take advantage of our good nature, and we'll be wiped out. We're a motorcycle club, not a fuckin' scout troupe. And that's the way I'm gonna run things. Here are my priorities. First, we get armed. I know we've got a stash of weapons for when shit gets bad, but we need more. A shit-ton more. Not just pistols. We need assault rifles. We need 'nades. We need fucking RPGs. We need respect."

"How we gonna get all that?" That was Crank, at the front of the room. His arms were crossed, and his body language was doubtful. Still, Crank seemed to be seriously considering Dog's ideas.

Rainer suspected that Dog's idea to arm themselves would go down well with the rest of the bikers. They still intercepted shipments of arms from the other gangs in the city from time to time, and it was important that the club stayed armed. Heck, they had quite a stash — RPGs, automatics, even a bunch of frigging night-vision equipment that had at one point been army tech. Having said that, he questioned why it was exactly that Dog thought that procuring a bunch of firearms was the top priority for the club.

He had the feeling that it wouldn't stop at just buying the guns. No doubt, Dog would sell a few of them, too. And that spelled trouble. Rainer thought a much better policy would be to watch for gun deals between other, more criminal organizations, and stop them being completed. That's what the club had done in the past.

"We'll get the damn guns any way we can," Dog said to cheers. "Buy, borrow, or steal. Way I see it, they're better off in our hands than in the hands of someone else. Like I said, we're an outlaw motorcycle club, not a bunch of girl guides selling cookies."

A bunch of people said, "Right," and "Fuckin' A."

"When we're armed, we take control of the drugs in this city."

This got Rainer even more worried. He glanced at Esme, and his mind went immediately to the other Littles affiliated with the club. The thought of them even being in the vicinity of narcotics made his skin crawl.

"Out of the question," Baron said, shaking his head.

"I'm not talking about dealing, Big Man," Dog said, making a calming gesture. "I'm talking about control. Safety. Security. People are gonna buy drugs no matter what, right? So, we make sure that the

drugs coming into New York are pure. We make sure they're safe. I
don't want people overdosing because of shoddy merchandise."

There were nods of approval, but, once again, Rainer wasn't buying
it. It sounded very much like a platform for dealing to him. Plus, as far
as he was concerned, there was no such thing as a safe drug.

"You're talking about setting up some kinda drug testing lab?"
Baron asked, doubt obvious in his voice.

"If that's what it takes, sure."

More positive sounds from the group.

"I want to move this club to where it should be. Respected by the
criminal organizations in the city and feared by the cops."

"Feared?"

There was a gasp. Esme had asked the question.

Dog screwed up his mouth. "Rainer," he said, quietly, "out of re-
spect for you, I agreed to you bringing your Old Lady to this meeting.
But so help me, it's not okay for a woman to speak at a meeting of the
MC. Frankly, I want to ban chicks from The Den altogether."

Rainer subconsciously made a fist under the table.

"Sorry, Daddy," Esme whispered. "I just—"

"Don't worry, babygirl," Rainer said. His brain was working at a
thousand miles an hour. Ahead of him, he saw the trajectory that the
club could take. Dipping its toe into shady dealings, before inevitably
taking a decidedly criminal path. He had a vision of people leaving,
and others — very different others — joining. Slowly, the club would
be taken over by people who didn't care about Littles, who didn't care
about standing up for vulnerable people.

The club had started as a way to give toys and games to needy, hos-
pitalized kids, and to protect vulnerable Littles. It was unconscionable
to him that it become a criminal organization. That feeling — that
intense, overwhelming desire to protect Esme — it wasn't just her that

he needed to protect. It was *all* the members of the MC, whether Little or Big. Rainer looked at Baron, who nodded at him.

Then, he stood up. There were murmurs of interest around the room.

"Dog, Drifters, I'm standing for President."

Dog looked as though he had been slapped across the mouth. "Whaddya mean?"

"I mean I'm going to do what Marcus wanted. I'm going to step up to the plate." He looked at Esme. "I'm gonna accept my fate."

"Too late," Dog said. "It's against the damn rules."

"Bullshit. There are no fucking rules. What are we, Dog, a bunch of goody-goody girl scouts?"

There was a roll of laughter around the bar.

"So, what's *your* vision for the club?" Dog said. "We just roll over and agree to get fucked by every damn hustler in the city?"

"No," said Rainer. "I don't know what my vision is. But that's the point. It shouldn't be my vision. It should be for the club to decide." An idea came to him, fully formed, as though it was the most obvious, easy thing in the world. "We'll ride. Together. The whole club. After I'm elected, we go on the most epic, awesome road trip of our lives. And together, we find the soul of the club, right where it should be. On the road."

There were cheers, there was applause. And in the middle of it all, Dog, with a face like murder.

"Alright, Rainer. Alright. You can stand. But right now, we need to talk," Dog said. "Just club members. Without the Littles."

"It's okay, Daddy, we'll play in the romp room," Esme said. She gestured toward Sophia, Molly, and the four other Littles who were dotted around the room.

As they left the room, Rainer felt something. The hand of destiny, resting on his shoulder.

The romp room was so new that the plastic it was covered in still had that strange, chemical scent. The place was covered in soft play equipment. There was a jukebox for music, and there were disco lights for the dancing.

The original Den, out in Albany, hadn't had a romp room, so Littles who visited tended to get bored. This place though, was a million times more fun and Little-friendly than the first bar ever had been.

Esme bent at the middle, with her butt poking up high into the sky, and her hands planted firmly on the ground. She shifted her weight from foot to foot, feeling the earth beneath her as it grounded her.

"Then what I do next is," she grunted, "I lift up my left leg." She transitioned into three-legged dog pose, hooking her left leg over, and feeling the burn in her core.

There were snuffles of effort around the room as the other littles copied her moves.

"It's impossible!" huffed Sophia, then a moment later there was a shriek, and she fell down, planting her face on the soft mat beneath.

"You can do it," Esme said, walking up to her.

They'd started out putting on some tunes and dancing around like the bunch of fun-loving Littles they were, but when a more peaceful, meditative song had come on the playlist, Esme had naturally transitioned into static poses.

Yoga poses.

Before too long, some of the other Littles were copying along, tittering a little, but still taking it relatively seriously.

It was only when she was adjusting Sophia's leg and helping her to balance when Esme realized what was going on.

All eyes were on her.

She was teaching a yoga class.

There was an instant burn in her cheeks, and a prickly sweat broke out across her body.

"Are you okay?" Sophia asked.

Esme's mouth had gone dry. Why did she have to get like this? Why could she not stand to have people look at her?

"I just need to go," she said, the panic rising.

"Potty?"

"Yeah, sure," she said, thankful that Sophia had helped her with the lie.

As she walked to the door, she felt a strong flashback. All those faces looking at her. Judging her. Thinking that she should have done something to stop the awful, awful thing that had happened. Tears wet her eyes, and she felt sobs catching in her throat.

She raised her hand to the door, but to her surprise, Rainer pushed it open.

"Hey," he said, clearly not expecting her to be right there.

"Hey."

He's gonna think I'm such a cry baby.

"Sweetheart?" He was clearly concerned. Then, to her infinite surprise, he asked, "Can I hold you?"

Every part of it shocked her. He cared about her. He wanted to hold her. He respected her enough to ask.

She nodded, and he wrapped her in his arms. The smell of musk and man was so much that she almost forgot herself. He was so much taller than her that her head rested on his chest. Deep inside, she heard his heart, thumping calmly, slowly, and she felt her own heart relax, matching his beat.

"You ready to go?" he whispered.

She nodded.

"Good. We've got a lot to talk about."

CHAPTER EIGHT

I T WAS DARK IN here. There was a candle on the table between them. The light flickered. Every time it shifted, Rainer's face was lit from a different angle, making him look infinitely handsome, impossibly deep.

He arched an eyebrow. "Bet you didn't think I'd be the kind of person to keep candles in the house."

"I'll admit that no, I didn't."

"I find them useful from time to time."

"For what?"

He considered this for a moment. "I'll show you one day. If you're lucky."

"Hmmph. Then I'll never get to see."

On the bike ride back to his place, Esme had held on so tightly to Rainer's back that it felt like he was hugging her right back. He was fast becoming her happy place. Being close to his immense physical form had a calming effect on her that she'd never experienced with any man before.

"You'll see. Don't worry. I thought a candle might help us be calm. I saw you looking a little sad in the romp room. That's a hectic place. Wanted this to be the opposite."

"That's nice."

"Want to tell me why you were sad?"

Esme screwed up her mouth, and — under the table — screwed up her fists, too.

"Hard to explain. I was doing yoga. People were joining in. I just... don't like people looking at me."

"You're a streamer, though."

"That's different. I can't see their faces."

Rainer nodded. "Makes sense."

"*You* seem okay with people looking at you."

Rainer sighed. "Feel like I made a mistake tonight."

"I was proud of you."

"Good."

Seeing him smile made her soul want to laugh with joy.

"Dog's mean," she said, sticking out her tongue. "I always thought he was mean."

"Lots of bikers are mean. Doesn't mean they're bad people."

"I know. I just mean... he's extra-mean. One time, he shouted at Josie."

Josie was a very soft-hearted, sweet-as-a-button Little who'd hung around the MC for a very long time. Esme really liked Josie, and the time that Dog had shouted at her — because she'd been sitting in his seat — had really stuck in her mind.

"You know, that is a very shi... shi... *bad* thing that he did. Little Josie doesn't have a bad bone in her body. You know, that's kind of why I decided to stand."

"Josie?"

"Not directly. It's more like... since I've been getting to know you, something's opened up in me. In my heart. I can't stand the thought of people suffering. I just have this feeling that if Dog becomes the Prez of the club, then people will suffer. Not just the club members, but the

Littles affiliated with the club, too. I don't want to let that happen. I believe it's our duty to protect vulnerable people at all costs."

Esme felt her heart swell as he spoke. "That feeling is because of me?"

"You know it is."

"Well. That makes me feel... all melty and gooey inside like a s'more."

His eyes fixed hers. In the flickering candlelight, it was like looking into the eyes of some benign giant.

"Esme, you and me, we're two halves of a whole. Do you feel it?"

She bit her lip. Nodded.

Rainer continued. "I struggle with giving in to fate. You struggle with fighting against it. I know we can help each other."

Without even feeling as though she was doing it, Esme's hand found Rainer's under the table. The touch was light to begin with, and she felt a profound energy surge through her as he returned it with his own. As he held her gently, her body thrummed with anticipation.

"I think we can, too, Daddy," she replied, feeling her chest rise and fall in time to some unheard, ancient rhythm.

It was unstoppable. There was something pushing her forward, moving her toward him. And as she moved, he did too. His hand moving up her arm, slowly, brushing her bare skin, caressing her upper arm, resting on her shoulder.

She was inches from him — centimeters. His eyes burned into hers as he pulled her onto his lap and then...

They kissed. It was soft, but just for a moment. As they communicated that — yes — they wanted, needed this to happen, and then, the gentleness gave way to hunger. He was passionate, demanding from the first, and as he held her more tightly, she realized for a moment that even if she wanted to, she couldn't break his grip.

Then she eased, let him take control, let him push his tongue into her mouth, and she met that fierce passion with a fire of her own.

And when it was over, she was panting. "Fuck."

"What did my Little girl just say?"

Her eyes widened. "I said frick?"

"Cussing *and* lying. Not a good start, young lady. How convenient that you're already on Daddy's lap."

"But Daddy, we haven't s-signed a contract," she said. She desperately wanted him to spank her, but — of course — at the same time, she was terrified of getting spanked.

"Fine. Your safeword is 'red.' Do you consent to me spanking you?"

"Yes," she said instantly. "Arrgghh. Damn me for being so turned on right now."

"You're turned on?" His grin was irritatingly huge.

"Maybe a little bit."

"And you said 'damn.'"

Her mouth formed a perfect 'o' shape. "You are so annoying."

"That's definitely an extra spank young lady. No matter how turned on you are. Now get over my knee."

She couldn't believe this was happening. Esme was desperate for it, but she wasn't prepared for how intense things had gotten between them, and how fast. It was like being fired out of a cannon — a very pretty, exciting, beautiful cannon, but a cannon, nonetheless.

Esme decided that, on balance, the best way to avoid too much extraneous spanking was to submit, so she twisted around so that she was bent over his lap.

"Good girl."

The words, said in Rainer's rich baritone gave her an instant shot of dopamine. She wanted to hear those words a lot more.

A moment later, his strong fingers ripped her skirt and panties down.

"Fuck, girl, your ass looks incredible in the candlelight." She felt his hand squeeze her buttock. Her pussy, which was already wet with lust, dampened even more.

"Daddy, what's that I feel poking into me?" It was a naughty thing to ask, but she just couldn't help herself.

There was a rustle below, and then Rainer showed her something.

Esme burst out laughing. It was Om Baby. Of course it was Om Baby.

"Nope. Not my cock." Rainer shifted a little underneath her.

Esme's eyes widened as something else, something harder, thicker, and a lot bigger prodded into her.

He whispered in her ear. "That's my cock."

Before she could react, the first spank came. A stinger — a wretched, painful, stinger of a spank, right on the underside of her buttocks. She winced and already felt her eyes start to water.

When the second came, she wished that she had a gag she could stuff between her teeth. She groaned with the pain of it, then, moments later, sighed at the waved of pleasure. With the third, fourth, fifth, she ground her pussy down into his thigh, trying to mitigate the agony with ecstasy.

"Five more, dirty girl," he grunted, before making good on his promise.

By the time he was finished, her ass was positively glowing.

Holy fuck. That was the best a spanking had ever felt in her life. He'd spanked her so dang hard it was like her soul was stinging from it.

"That was intense," she said.

"You feeling good?"

"Mmmhmm. So good, Daddy. So good I'm tempted to cuss again."
He traced his fingertips over her aching buttocks, soothing them with
the gentleness of his touch.

"You know that I won't spank you if you do it again, right? Cussing
ain't a one-way ticket to pleasure land."

"I guessed as much." She let out a humph.

"Still, if you thought that was intense, you're gonna enjoy what's
coming next."

Esme felt a pang of nerves as she imagined what they were going to
do. "What's coming next?"

"We're gonna work out what your fate is, Little one."

He shifted her so that she was sitting up. It hurt so badly to be sitting
like this, but she knew that's exactly why he'd done it. He was a stern
Daddy — she was learning that very quickly.

"Come on, let's get to know each other."

The notebook lay open empty in front of Esme. Rainer had turned
on the lights for this. He didn't want his Little to be straining her eyes
to see as she write.

"First," he said, "why don't you write your name on the front?"

"Like at school?"

"Right. Except this is gonna be more fun than school. Probably
learn a heck of a lot more here, too. I can only speak for myself, but the
only thing I learned in school was how to feel shi-bad about myself."

He was getting better at catching himself cussing.

"By the way," he said, as Esme scribbled her name — her full name, Esmeralda Adams — on the front of the notebook, "I decided that every time I cuss, I'm gonna put a dollar in a jar. Then, when we've got enough, I'll buy you a treat."

"Ooohhh, a treat! I'mma make you cuss a whole bunch, Daddy."

"How?"

She gave him a filthy look, and — without warning — she pulled up her shirt. It was just for a second, but he caught sight of her generous, perfectly-formed breasts, supported by a hot pink bra.

"Holy fuck!" he exclaimed before he had time to think. Then, he added, "You're evil."

She did the perfect impersonation of a witch's laugh.

"Now, what am I gonna write in here?"

"First off, I wanna say something important. Now, obviously, I'm attracted to you."

"What?" Esme said, clearly being playful. "Seriously? Daddy! I'm shocked!"

"You know, some Daddies smack their Littles for sarcasm."

"Eeek. Do you?"

"Not currently," he grinned. "The point is, I'm attracted to you. I want to explore a romantic relationship with you. But I want to do it responsibly. And that means taking it slow."

"Uggggghhhh," she groaned. "Slow is boring. I like it fast."

Damn, it would be so good to fuck her. She wanted it. He wanted it. He could be inside her within minutes.

No Rainer. That's not the way. You know it's not the way.

"I know it's frustrating. For both of us. But I promise you that this is going to get intense, and we don't want to throw extra vulnerability into the mix. Understand?"

She nodded, looking serious.

"Good. Now, I want you to write down things that you love."

"Easy peasy."

"And I want you to write down the things that you're scared of. And the reasons that you're scared of them. This way, it'll be easier than talking to me about them."

Instantly, Esme's face was full of anxiety. "I don't know if I can."

"Do you want to try?"

Rainer had hoped that Esme might be alright doing this. If she wasn't, though, he had another trick up his sleeve.

"I can try the things I love first."

"Sure."

He watched her as she started to write, her tongue occasionally poking out her mouth with the effort of it. Her handwriting was sweet, neat, and considered, and she took her time with every letter. Each word and sentence filled his heart with happiness.

The sunshine.

Food — any food.

Feeling loved.

Feeling like I'm being a good girl.

The movie Hocus Pocus.

The book James and the Giant Peach.

Reading and being read to.

Unicorns, rainbows, general multicolored stuff.

Water. Being under it.

Feeling clean.

The smell of sandalwood and sage.

Coloring carefully.

Taking my time.

I love it when things just work out, but it doesn't happen very often.

Bangs – I just wish I didn't look like my face was a window surround-ed by curtains when I have them.

Snow.

Christmas.

The list went on. She managed at least forty items.

"You've done so well. Any time you want to, you can add to it, and read through it when you need reminding of all the good stuff in life."

"There's one more thing," she said, sticking out her tongue again.

I love writing this list.

At the end of the sentence, she drew a little heart.

"Now, how do you feel about writing down what you don't like? I can leave you alone to do it if you feel embarrassed."

"No! Don't leave, Daddy. I like being with you."

"I like being with you, babygirl. Okay, well how about this? How about we write a list together of the things that Om Baby doesn't like?"

"Hmmm. That could work."

"You can dictate, and I'll write them down."

"Okay," she said, her eyes brightening. "Let's try."

"So, what's the first thing?"

Esme handed Rainer the pen, her fingers accidentally brushing his as she did so.

"First, put, 'Om Baby hates it when she can't hold a yoga pose.'"

"Perfect."

CHAPTER NINE

T HE LIST THAT THEY wrote that day didn't stay in the notebook for long. Om Baby's fears and dislikes became a constant
touchstone for the two of them, and as they worked together to regress
Esme, they talked often about fears.

Rainer bought a big blackboard, and chalked the list up in large,
bright letters, then hung it from the wall. He wanted Esme to see that
the more you faced your fears, the less scary they became.

"Om Baby?" Rainer asked the stuffie, a couple days after they came
up with the initial list.

"Yes, Daddy Rainer?" Om Baby answered, using Esme — who she
called her secretary — to communicate with him.

"One of the things on your list of fears is: people watching you."

"Om Baby doesn't like that," Om Baby replied.

"Let's imagine for a moment that people were watching you right
now."

It was the part of the day when Esme was doing her daily yoga
practice. Right now, she was in tree pose — Rainer was very quickly
getting to learn the various stances and poses as Esme loved to explain
what her body was doing while she practiced. She stood on one foot,
and, with her other leg bent, she pressed the foot into her inner thigh.
Her hands reached above her head, stretching up to the sky.

"Scary," said Om Baby.

Rainer had found that using Om Baby to chat to him about her innermost fears was a powerful tool for Esme. He knew one thing for certain: she'd been through something terrible when she was younger, and she found it almost impossible to talk about it. At least when she was being Om Baby, that part of her was a little more accessible.

"What's the worst thing that could happen?" he asked the stuffie.

He'd been slowly building up to this question. Over the past couple days, he'd asked Esme about other, less scary fears. Things like Om Baby's supposed fear of the dark, and of "big cats" (which actually was just a fear of regular house cats). Esme's replies had been fairly light-hearted, but he was sure she knew that they were getting ready to tackle something big together.

"I could make a fool of myself. Or worse." She paused for a moment. "Something terrible could happen. Something that I could have averted. And everyone could see. And they'd know that I'm too scared to ever do anything."

"How would you feel if that happened?"

Esme put her foot down on the ground, and Rainer walked up to her, letting his palms rest on her shoulder blades. He gently rubbed her smooth skin, trying to beam warmth and calm into her.

"I'd feel crushed," she said, moaning quietly with pleasure.

"Do you think that you might be able to put on a little show, just for me?"

"A show?" She sounded confused.

"Some Littles like to put on shows. It could be anything. Singing. Painting. Acting. Anything. I'd love to watch you."

"Sounds scary."

Rainer had never met anyone who was such a perfect mixture of adorable and sexy before. Her body was like something out of a dream.

Athletic, but curvaceous. Lithe, but soft. The swoop of her breasts and the deep curve of her hips was so intoxicating, it felt like he was walking around with a semi basically all the time he was with her. When she was dressed for yoga, he could barely contain himself. Her tight-fitting clothes left almost nothing to her imagination.

And then there was her face.

Oh... her face.

Such big, expressive, emerald-green eyes. Pouty, dark pink lips, like over-sized cherries. That cute little chin, with that sexy dimple in its center. The way that her glossy, black hair fell across her face sometimes. The way she tucked it behind her ears. Even her fucking ears were perfect. Her left was piercing free, but her right was studded with silver hoops; two in the lobe, one in the tragus and a slim one in her helix, too. She was everything he'd ever wanted and more.

"It might be scary," he admitted. "But fear is good. Means that you're pushing yourself. You won't be in your comfort zone anymore. And the only way to grow is to get right out of your comfort zone."

She sighed. "I think I know what kind of show to do."

"Oh?"

She nodded. "It's something I used to do a lot when I was a kid. Before I got into yoga. I hope I can still pull it off for you. Hope I can still impress!"

"I'm gonna be impressed with anything. For me, the impressive thing is that you're trying it. You've already done the hard part by committing."

He could see that she was nervous, so he planted a kiss on her forehead. He loved the smell of her skin. He'd noticed, ever since going through the list of things she loved, that she had the sweet smell of sandalwood and cinnamon. Obviously, it was the scent she chose, but it was delicious, and the temptation to gently bite her tender flesh was strong whenever he was near.

"You smell good enough to eat, Little one," he growled into her ear, feeling lusty chemicals flood his brain.

"Don't eat me just yet, Daddy," she replied. "Otherwise I won't be able to do my show."

Somehow, he managed to pull back. "Well, alright then. I'll save you for later."

Why had she agreed to do this? Of all the dumb things, she had to put herself into exactly the kind of situation that she'd been trying to avoid for her entire adult life.

The trouble was, she trusted him.

She really trusted him.

There was something magic about Rainer. It was the magic of reliability. The magic of being dependable.

If he said he was gonna do something, he did it. Always.

If he said that he was going to *try* cooking a meal that he'd never cooked before, and that it might not turn out great, that's exactly what would happen. Like when he made pancakes for breakfast this morning, and they'd been a little less fluffy than would have been ideal.

If he said that he would home at a certain time, that was the exact time he'd be back. Not a minute early, not a minute late.

If he promised not to laugh at your coloring in, no matter how many times you'd gone over the lines, and no matter how horrendous your color combinations were, he would be completely stony-faced as he said, sincerely, "I love it."

Esme knew that she could rely on him. So, when he asked her to put on a show, she'd barely even considered it before accepting the challenge. She knew he wouldn't judge. She knew he'd be supportive.

Didn't make it any less nerve-wracking. Didn't make her feel any less dumb for what she'd decided to show him.

But still, she knew what to expect.

"Are you ready out there?" she asked. Her body was trembling. She'd been limbering up for at least ten minutes, trying to push herself so that she was ready for this.

"Ready as I'll ever be," Rainer said.

Well, Esme, here goes nothing.

She hit the play button on her phone, and "Toxic" by Britney Spears started to play. It was tinny, and the bass was almost non-existent, but having the music on made her feel a little more confident.

Esme walked in slowly. She was wearing a *very* revealing outfit. Well, it was less of an outfit and more of a leotard — flesh-pink, like a second skin.

Instantly, Rainer's eyes widened. She wondered exactly what kind of show he thought he was about to get.

"When I was a young woman," she said, stepping in daintily, "I was into contortionism."

The music swelled, and Esme eased into her first pose — the splits. She felt discomfort as she moved down, but it was nowhere near as bad as she was expecting. It was amazing just how much her body remembered. The yoga had definitely helped, but without her original contortionist training, she wouldn't be able to do this.

It was impossible not to feel the sexual tension of the situation. She pushed her pussy down into the ground, and Rainer gaped as she started to gently bounce up and down, pushing the stretch further with each breath.

"Holy f...iddlesticks," Rainer muttered under his breath.

Esme couldn't help but smile.

He'd never seen anything like it. The shapes she was making seemed impossible. Pulling her legs over her head, bending her body so acutely that she looked like a human pretzel.

He sat there, watching her, with the music pounding, and he felt his cock lengthening and thickening in his pants, almost like it was struggling to get free.

She was so... fucking... bendy.

It was impossible not to imagine all the shapes the two of them could make, together. Her legs wrapped around *his* head. Her legs spread so wide, making so much space for him. Her muscles were strong, her tendons supple. He could only imagine how welcoming her pussy would be.

At one point, she put her foot up on a chair and did the splits onto it in such a way that she really looked like she was gonna snap. But there was no effort on her face – just a happy, calm smile that was making his stomach do somersaults.

"How are you doing that?" he asked.

"I don't know."

"Does it hurt?"

She bit her lip and looked at him with those vulnerable green eyes. "It feels good, Daddy." Her eyes flashed to his crotch. She had to have seen his cock there, straining against his pants.

Esme stood, letting him marvel for just a second at the insane sexual energy she was pushing out, and then, she bent over backward and grabbed hold of her ankles. All he could do was stare at her in awe.

By the end of the performance, a sheen of sweat was visible on her. There was a flush in her cheeks. Somehow, it made her look even more beautiful.

She bowed. Rainer clapped.

"No exaggeration. That was the most amazing thing I've ever seen."

Esme's eyes widened in appreciation. "Thank you, Daddy. I did good?"

"You did incredible. Makes me wonder how many other secret skills you've got tucked away in that amazing body of yours."

She took an exploratory step toward him. "You think my body is amazing?"

"I think everything about you is amazing."

There was nothing he wanted to do right now than feel that body push up against him. There had been times when her ample breasts had been squashed down into the ground, when he could practically *feel* the juiciness of her.

"That's nice."

She was right there. Right in front of him. All he had to do was pull her into him and *enjoy*.

"Well, you seem to have overcome your fear."

"Oh yeah," she said. "*That* was the point of this, wasn't it?"

"Right. And it's given me some interesting ideas."

Her eyes widened. "What sort of ideas?"

Like how you'd look bent over with my cock between those soft lips.

"Ideas to help you face up to your fears even more. Ideas which are gonna help you wrestle control of your life back from fate."

He'd made the transfer of rent to her landlord a couple days ago. But his plan was to make sure that she was fully self-sufficient by the time of next month's payment.

"Thank you, Daddy," she said. And she leaned over, deep and low, and planted a single, wet kiss on his forehead. When she straightened, it was obvious through her leotard that it wasn't just her mouth that was wet.

"Girl, you're too much."

How was he meant to do this without fucking her? He was going to have to be as strong as she would have to be flexible.

CHAPTER TEN

I T WAS THE NEXT morning, over a steaming hot pot of coffee, that the real work began.

"I really need this coffee," she said.

"I can tell," Rainer replied. There was something about the look he gave her. Something knowing.

But he couldn't know. Could he?

Esme had been up all night. She played over the sexy show she'd put on for Rainer about a billion times in her head, remembering how her body felt as she stretched her legs up and round her head. Her pussy had practically been on fire, her nipples had been hard as tacks.

In the night, she'd explored her body, as she'd imagined a very different way the show could have ended. Her fingertips parted her pussy lips as she thought of Rainer splitting her leotard, pulling it apart and feasting on her wet sex with that hot tongue of his.

She pinched her nipples as she fantasized about his cock, a clearly visible lump of hard lust, springing free of his pants. She'd imagined acting surprised, and he'd be even more turned on, unable to stop himself from sliding his full length into her supple, accommodating pussy.

Esme came over and over again in the night, stifling her cried with her fist, praying that the walls in Rainer's spartan apartment were thick enough to muffle her moans of pleasure.

"Good coffee," she said, smiling nervously.

"Just what you need after an unsettled night."

Memories of the power of her orgasms flowed through her. She did everything she could not to blush, but, of course, she blushed nonetheless.

"So, what's this plan you've got?"

Rainer raised an eyebrow. "Changing the subject to planning for the future. I never thought I'd see the day."

"Well, you must be rubbing off on me." Then, realizing what she'd said, "I mean, your attitude must be rubbing off on me."

God fucking damn it I would love you to rub off on me.

If Rainer could hear what was going on in her brain, she'd be smacked constantly. Which didn't actually sound that bad...

"Don't worry, Little one, I know what you meant. Well, this morning we're going to be writing up a daily routine, and a set of rules, to help you take back control."

"Sounds good."

He took a sip of his coffee. "Now, I know you've been relying on your streaming for income. Not a bad way to live, even if there are downsides."

"You mean the whole stalker issue?" She absentmindedly twirled her hair around her finger.

"Yes. That's exactly what I mean. I'm not the biggest fan of streaming for that reason. But, if it's what you want to do, then I'll support you one hundred percent."

She couldn't help but feel her heart flutter in her chest. It had been so long since someone — anyone — had taken this much interest in her life. It made her feel unbelievably cared for. It also made her feel kinda like she didn't deserve it.

"If you decide you do want to pursue streaming as a career, I'll work with you to make sure you're safe. Then you won't need to worry about guys turning up at your doorstep, demanding personal tarot readings."

"That would be nice."

"But I also get the feeling that maybe, if you could, there's something else you'd rather be doing."

Well, he was entirely right.

"Maybe."

"So tell me. If you could do anything in the world, anything at all, what would you do?"

She didn't miss a beat. "Chocolate tester."

Rainer let out a deep laugh that was so resonant it tickled her tummy. "I deserved that. Okay, let me rephrase the question. If you could pick any *realistic* career, what would you pick?"

"Yoga instructor."

"Thanks for your honesty. Don't worry, if you want, you can be an amateur chocolate tester."

"Really?"

"Course. It's a Daddy's responsibility to make his Little girl's dreams come true. I'll hook you up with some rare candies to wrap those luscious lips around. We can come up with a scoring sheet, too."

"Ooohhh, a candy scoring sheet! All my friends told me not to date a biker, and now I know why." She was teasing, but there was a thrill to it. They *were* dating, weren't they? They'd still only kissed the once, and even though she ached for him, it felt like they had a long road ahead of them.

"Right. It's all guns, drugs, and candies with us assholes," he joked. Then, he took out a sheet of paper. "So, it's time. We're gonna make a plan that's gonna craft you into a yoga instructor."

She bit her lip and wrung her hands together. "What if I just can't do it? What if I can't overcome my fear?"

"Honey, I believe in you, but I'm not going to force you to do anything you don't want to do. My feeling is that you're gonna rise to the challenge. But if you decide that it's too scary, and that it's doing you more harm than good, then I *promise* we'll revisit this plan. The last thing I want to do is cause you distress. Understand?"

She nodded.

"Good." He pulled the cap off the pen. "Now, let's get planning!"

It was a daunting schedule.

"I've never tried anything like this. Not since school."

"Not much will change, day to day. You were already on a daily routine that was similar to this."

"Yeah, but now it's all written down. Feels like I have to do it." Her heart had been fluttering the whole time they'd been organizing the plan, mainly because she knew that after the plan, they were going to be making the rules and punishments official, too.

"Now, Esme, I wanted to ask you, how do you feel about living here, with me, for a while?"

"Really?" Esme's heart almost stopped from excitement. No-one had ever asked her to live with him before. Obviously, this was a bit of an unusual situation. It wasn't like Rainer was asking her to move in permanently, or because he loved her. But still, it had to mean something, didn't it?

"Of course. I know it's a big step, and I'll completely understand if you'd rather take more slowly. It'd just be easier logistically."

"Sure. Logistically."

"Right. Plus, there's the fact that I'm crazy about you and I want to spend all my time with you."

Esme's mouth hung open in surprise. "You're crazy about me?"

"Can't you tell, babygirl? I feel very, very strongly about you."

She was lost in his warm eyes again. Felt like the world was spinning. "Well... that's nice."

His grin made her whole body hum with pleasure. "Good. So, what do you think?"

"I'll stay here. Might need to pick up a few things from my place."

"Course. Whatever you need. Leave whatever you want here. Treat it like your place. Well. Almost." He took out a fresh piece of paper. "Rule one: everything has its place. We're going to be living in an organized, tidy home. Understood?"

"Yes, Daddy."

"I'm going to be strict about this. We don't just tidy once a week. No. It's a mindset. We deserve to live in a tidy home, so it will be tidy always. We put things away after we use them. If we spill something, we clean it up. With me?"

This was going to be a challenge for her.

"I'll do my best."

"I know it's going to be hard, but if I'm going to be your Daddy long-term, then this is a rule that we're going to have to stick to. And my punishment will be strict."

She gulped. Even thinking back to the painful spanking she'd received at his hands made her quiver and shake.

"Rule number two: do as Daddy says. It's a simple one, but it's all about trust. I have your very best interests at heart. I have done ever since you puked up all over my favorite t-shirt."

"That was your favorite?" It had just been a simple white t-shirt as far as she could remember.

"Mmmhmm. Don't remind me."

"Eeek. I think I can obey you, though. I trust you. I really do." She reached forward and squeezed his hand.

"I'm glad. Trust means everything to me. I promise I'll never lie to you."

"I promise that, too."

"That's a good rule. No lies — actually, let's phrase it more positively."

He wrote: "We will always be honest with each other."

A few more rules went down without too much discussion.

Always let Daddy know where you are.

Always shower after a workout.

No cussing.

Then, Rainer asked, "I'd like to be in charge of your pleasure. How does that sit with you?"

"As in—"

"As in no naughtiness without telling me. And absolutely no orgasms without my say-so."

She screwed up her mouth, then said something that surprised her. "Daddy, last night I was thinking about you, and I touched myself and made myself come three times." Her hand shot up to her mouth. "Did I just say that?"

He paused. "Seems that way."

For a moment, she wasn't sure if he was going to be angry or happy. Thankfully, it was the latter.

"Thank you for telling me, sweetheart. You just made me feel very good."

Esme mumbled something under her breath.

"What was that?"

"I said I... respect you, Daddy."

Esme watched with glee as Rainer struggled to keep a big, dumb grin off his face.

"Glad to hear it. I knew something was up in your room. I kept hearing these little... snuffles. At first, I thought someone had broken in."

She was blushing so hard that it felt like her face was buzzing.

"I'm sorry. I know it was naughty."

"Well, in the future, it'll mean a punishment. But seeing as we hadn't agreed on the rules, I'll let you off on this occasion."

They worked through the rest of the rules together. They were mostly to do with safety (making sure to lock her door if she was going to be home alone) and sticking to the schedule (using her phone's calendar to set up alarms to remind her of her schedule). The time flew by, but before she knew it, it was lunch time.

"What are we having?"

"I thought I'd make you a smoothie."

"Wait," Esme said, "*you* have a smoothie-maker?"

"How else am I gonna get my daily green goddess fix?"

For a moment, she thought he was being serious. He had such a dry sense of humor. There were times that she couldn't quite work out whether he was being serious or not.

"Wolf gave it to me after I helped him refurbish the Den. It was an old one he didn't need anymore. Kind of a joke. He knows what I think about fruit and vegetables."

"What do you think?"

"Um... they're great?"

"I can see why you want honesty all the time, Daddy. You're a terrible liar!"

"True. Now, let me fix you up something, then you're to get on with your afternoon's schedule while I head to the shop. I can't spend *all* my time here, as much as I'd like to."

Powered by the surprisingly delicious, and very healthy-tasting smoothie, Esme got a lot of stuff done that afternoon. Rainer had done a ton of research for her, and he'd left her with a series of TED talks and other YouTube videos to watch to help her with facing her fears.

Normally, she'd kick off her shoes and lie on her bed, before watching a vid on her phone and — probably — fall asleep before the end of it.

Not today, though.

First, she sat at the kitchen table. She took out a pad of paper, and, as the video played, she took notes. Like a good girl. It was the most writing she'd done since school, and it felt weirdly soothing. Honestly, all this self-care did. It was like a vacation into someone else's life. A vacation into a world in which she deserved to look after herself.

It felt good.

After she'd finished making the notes, and she'd watched the videos twice, it was time for yoga. She took a full hour, working through the kind of routine she'd love to be taught, giving her whole body a workout.

By the time Rainer was due back, Esme felt like a different person. She felt proud of herself.

Esme could feel a shift. She was taking control of her life. All it had needed was a Daddy to control *her*.

It felt good to be a good girl, and when Rainer came home, she was excited to show him what she'd done.

But there was a little part of her that even more excited to think what might be happening if she'd been a *bad girl* that day.

CHAPTER ELEVEN

FOUR DAYS, AND NOT so much as a kiss.

"Four days?" Kelly looked at her, indignant. "Girl, that's a long time to be living with someone without even kissing them."

Esme was desperate to take things further with Rainer, but she didn't want to jeopardize anything by pushing her luck. "I know, I know. It sounds like he's not into me, but—"

"He's into you. No question."

"How do you know?"

"Um, have you seen yourself lately? You're a gosh-darn s-bomb!"

"Did you seriously just say s-bomb, instead of sex-bomb? Are you sure you're not a Little, Kelly?"

Kelly looked deeply embarrassed. "You know I don't like to cuss."

They were sitting together in a coffee shop in Brooklyn. Rainer had worked time into Esme's schedule for socializing. He was very clear that he thought a full social life was crucial for a Little.

It was good to see Kelly. Even though Esme was loving spending time with Rainer, it was good to just talk to someone who wasn't into either the age play lifestyle or the world of Harley Davidsons. Sometimes you needed a friend to help you see the world more clearly.

"But sex isn't even a cuss word! It's like, a science word. It's technical vocabulary."

Kelly took a sip of her drink. Obviously, she was just drinking an unsweetened black coffee. No creamer. No calories. But she wasn't doing it to deny herself – Kelly just seemed to genuinely prefer her food and drink healthy.

"I've been meaning to ask you. How do you know if you're a Little?"

Interesting. Very interesting.

"Hmm, that's a hard question to answer. I've only got my own experience to go off. I didn't really *know* for a long time."

"You didn't know when you were a kid?"

Esme shook her head. "When I was a kid, I was just a kid." She realized it sounded a little dumb, but it was the only way she could put it.

She thought back to those days. The endless summers, playing with her sister. The love of her parents. The joy of feeling as though life could only ever get better, bigger, more full of experience.

All of that had changed in a moment.

"It was later. After... something bad happened. I just knew that I had unfinished business with my childhood."

There was sympathy in Kelly's eyes. She knew that Esme had been through a very tough time, even if she didn't know the exact details of her experience. Esme hadn't really opened up to anyone about it.

"That makes sense."

"But I think it's different for everyone. Littles have different needs and different reasons for getting involved in the lifestyles. It's a spectrum, you know?"

Kelly looked around conspiratorially, as if to check whether anyone was listening, or even close enough to listen.

"Is it always, like... you know, to do with 's...'?"

Esme couldn't help but smile. "Sex, you mean?"

Kelly put a finger to her lips and shushed Esme, who giggled like an idiot.

"It's not, actually, always s-related. Some people just like to relax in a Little mindset and feel cuddly and cute and well looked after. Some people like to have fixed boundaries and discipline, but it doesn't cross over."

"Does it cross over for you?"

"Kinda," Esme said. "Like, I can feel sexy when I'm Little, but I don't like to fully go there while I'm in Little Space. But, you know, I find spanking sexy."

Kelly's face was about as pink as Esme had ever seen it.

"There's places you can go," Esme continued. "If you're interested in experimenting. I know a really good place in the Bronx."

"Oh," Kelly replied, looking flustered, "I'm just asking for a friend."

Esme gave her a look. "Well, I hope she knows that if she ever wants to talk to me about it, she's more than welcome."

"Thank you. Sorry to make this about me. I mean. About my friend."

They shared a look. "Don't worry," Esme said. "It's good to talk."

"You know what I think about the no-kiss situation?"

Esme sat back in her chair. The song changed — it was yet another of the bland, mindless muzak-style tracks that coffee shops like this always played. The type of music that Rainer would no doubt hate with a passion.

"What do you think about it?"

"You know how Rainer's been teaching you to take control of your life? Well, I think it's time you started to take control of the relationship."

"What do you mean?" Esme asked, suspiciously.

"Nothing bad! I just think that maybe, if you apply a little bit of naughtiness, you might be able to accelerate things."

"Break the rules?"

"Right. You know in the best yoga sessions, how you push yourself to the absolute limit? You know that good pain, that pain that means your body is changing, that pain that means you're becoming capable of new things? I think that's the pain you need to go through."

"So, what you're saying is, be a really naughty girl and get Daddy to spank me really, really hard?"

Kelly sighed. "You're impossible, you know that?"

"Impossibly great?"

"That's it. By the way, I've been meaning to tell you, whenever you feel ready to start teaching yoga, my studio is right there for you. Maybe we could even go into business together." Kelly reached over the table and clasped Esme's hand. "Wouldn't that be great?"

"Impossibly great," Esme grinned.

But deep inside, fear still bubbled away. She still had some way to go before the thought of standing in front of other people, telling them what to do didn't fill her with icy dread.

She could see the path ahead, though, and that was a first for her. She felt a thrill that took her right back — maybe the future could be better, bigger, more full of experience.

The coffee tasted of hope.

Rainer checked his watch for what felt like the millionth time this morning. Esme had gone to meet a good friend of hers, but was already fifteen minutes late in returning to his place.

She'll be fine. She probably just left it too late to get the subway. She's probably just enjoying spending time with her friend.

Rainer kept running over probable scenarios in his head, but he couldn't help feeling a sense of creeping dread.

Images of Esme, walking through New York, lost and scared, haunted him. He checked his watch again. She was seventeen minutes late now. He kept pacing around the kitchen. The lunch he'd prepared sat on the counter — bagels with cream cheese and smoked salmon, fresh green salad with vinaigrette, and a pot full of herbal tea.

In the short time they'd been together, Rainer had become quite an accomplished cook. He'd taken to reading recipe websites while he was meant to be working. It was important to him that Esme received delicious, nutritionally-balanced meals.

But maybe she didn't care about that.

Maybe Esme's friend had convinced her not to go back. Maybe he'd got things completely wrong and she just wasn't interested in him at all.

"Calm down, Rainer. Calm the fuck down."

He couldn't remember the last time he'd been this worried about anything. The feeling took him by surprise. He knew that he cared for Esme, but this was a different level. Such a vulnerable, raw feeling.

Please be okay. Please be okay.

To take his mind off the worry, he whipped out his phone and texted Baron.

Bro, would you punish a Little who's late for a date?

The reply came within seconds, almost as if Baron had been waiting for him.

A spank for each minute she's late, no question. You planning any campaigning for your Presidency bid?

In truth, Rainer had barely thought about the fact that he was running for President of the Drifters. All his thoughts had been consumed by helping Esme.

Nope. People know who I am. If they prefer me to Dog, that's great. If they don't, so be it. It's got to be club's decision.

He was trying to take a leaf from Esme's book by seeing what fate would serve. At the same time, he felt pretty sure that people would choose him over Dog. At least, he hoped that they would.

Baron sent another message.

Hmm. Dog is really going for it. Heard rumors he's smearing you.

Rainer scowled at his phone.

Let him fucking try. No one likes a shit-talker. I know the club.

He hoped that he had the right policy for this. It felt right to him — Marcus had picked him. It hadn't been his choice to run. Now he wanted to see if the rest of the club would pick him too, for who he was, not for some fake-ass leadership campaign. He'd see.

Just then, there was a very guilty-sounding knock at the door.

Thank fuck.

Rainer stormed to the front door, feeling a bizarre mixture of anger and relief. He wasn't quite sure how he was going to react when he saw Esme.

He pulled open the door. "What time do you call this, young lady?"

She looked up at him with the guiltiest, naughtiest expression on her face. "Oh? Am I late?"

Rainer knew that instant that she'd done it on purpose.

"Sweetheart," he said, more seriously than he'd been expecting, "you worried me sick."

Instantly, the naughty half-smile dropped away from her face. "I have?"

"Of course you have. No message to let me know that you were going to be late?"

"I... I... it was only a few minutes."

"Almost twenty."

She looked deeply ashamed. "I'm sorry, Daddy. I didn't mean to upset you. I just... I j—"

"You wanted to push your limits, didn't you?"

For a moment, it looked as though she was going to deny it, but she knew better than that.

"I'm sorry, Daddy."

It was so hard to see her face lined with sadness, but it was important that he let her know how worried he'd been. "I understand. Every Little girl needs boundaries. You're trying to figure out what kind of Daddy you're working with. It makes sense. But let me tell you, this is *not* a healthy way to test those boundaries. Going to bed later than normal or refusing to eat your greens is one thing, but this is completely different."

Esme was wringing her hands together and frowning deeply. There was something more going on, he could just tell. He was about to say something when Esme burst into tears. She sobbed big, ugly, heaving sobs.

"I'm sorry Daddy. I was s-stupid, so stupid."

"It's okay baby, I didn't mean to be so hard on you." He reached forward instinctively, pulling her close to him. "I was too hard, wasn't I?"

"No," she sniffed. "I deserve to be told off. I deserve punishment. I just... I just..."

"You can tell me, sugar. Anything."

"It was Kelly's idea. Kind of. Or at least, she put the idea in my head."

He was confused. "Kelly told you to be late?"

"No, she didn't. Oh, this is gonna make me sound so dumb."

"I won't judge."

There was a big sigh, and then Esme said, "I was worried you'd gone off me."

"What? What gave you that idea?"

"It's just, we only kissed once. I thought you'd changed your mind. Like, you didn't find me attractive. Or that since I started living with you, you found me annoying, or... or... too childish and silly." She was crying again now, her tears moistening Rainer's chest as he held her close to him.

"Babygirl, nothing could be closer to the truth."

"I thought that if I did something naughty, you might spank me again, and that might lead to more, and then..."

"I get it, sweetheart, I get it." He stroked her head. "You were feeling vulnerable, huh?"

"Big time! It's like my soul's on display!"

"You're not in trouble. Well, I mean, you're gonna get a punishment for being late — that's a given. But, I don't blame you for the way you're feeling. Sounds like I need to be more honest with you. More open. And maybe, after your punishment, I can make you feel good."

His hand strayed down, onto her butt. He gave a slight squeeze and felt her react to his touch. She felt so good in his arms. He never wanted to let go.

"You'd make me feel good down there?" she whispered.

"I'll make you feel good exactly where you need to feel good, babygirl," he replied.

Esme kissed his neck and nuzzled into him, making soft, snuffling sounds. "I want to be braver when I'm around you, Daddy. I want to be okay with being seen. With being me."

Rainer stroked her hair. "You deserve to be seen, darling. You're a superstar."

I love you, Esme.

He didn't say it, but it was there, at the center of his heart. Instead, he said: "Right now, though, it's time for your punishment."

CHAPTER TWELVE

E SME STARED AT THE cubicle ahead of her. She'd never felt this scared of a shower before.

"Is this absolutely necessary, Daddy?" she asked, her voice quavering.

"It is."

"It's just... I thought you might spank me. Or, or, or tie me up?"

Rainer stood with his arms crossed over his chest, a look of resolute determination on his face.

"You did something very serious today, Esme, so you're receiving a serious punishment. You made me worry that something terrible had happened to you. But you were also dishonest — you were late *on purpose*. You must never do that again. Ever. So, this punishment is designed to be memorable and unpleasant."

"I know but... a cold shower? What if I pass out?"

"You won't. But if, for some reason you *were* to pass out, I'd be right here to catch you."

"Hang on, you're going to be right here?"

Rainer nodded, looking amused. "Of course. Where else would I be?"

"But I'm gonna be naked. Nude. Totally bare."

"Right. Does that seem inappropriate to you? Remember that you have a safeword if you feel like the punishment get too much. I won't judge you for it, but if you wish to continue with me as your Daddy, I will have to devise an equally tough punishment."

The last thing she wanted was for him to stop. She found the idea of him seeing her naked to be very exciting – she just hoped that it wouldn't put him off her.

"No, I... like that you'll see me naked, Daddy."

"Thank you for your honesty, Little one."

"How long will I have to stay in the cold shower?"

"Two minutes should be enough."

"Two minutes?!" she practically shouted. "I'm gonna freeze my butt off!"

"We can make it two and a half if you like?"

"Eek! No! Two minutes is plenty."

Brrrr. Just thinking about the amount of cold water that would cascade out of the shower head was making her want to shiver. At least it was a nice-looking shower. Rainer had a bunch of nice stuff, actually. This bathroom looked like it had been designed by... well, a designer. Slate-gray tiles, polished chrome fittings, and a super-wide rain-style showerhead. For a badass biker, Rainer had good taste.

"Shall we get started?" he asked. "Clothes off, please."

She was wearing brown corduroy pants, and a purple-green tie-dye vest that fit her very tightly. But, in anticipation of a potential sexy time, she was also wearing the most sensual underwear she owned.

It was a hot pink peephole bra and a matching pair of crotchless panties. She'd bought them for herself as a treat/joke when she'd visited an adult store in Brooklyn with Sophia a couple months ago. They'd been looking for Little stuff. Sophia had bought a couple pacis and a sippy cup, but Esme had been more drawn to the sexy stuff. Sure, she'd bought a unicorn onesie, too, but that was for another time.

Point is, she felt embarrassed already about the prospect of Rainer seeing her sexy underwear.

"I should warn you I'm very slow at getting undressed," Esme said.

In response, Rainer slapped his hands together with such force Esme yelped.

"Message received, sir." She saluted to let him know she didn't want any further punishments, then, she undid her pants and wriggled out of them.

Rainer watched carefully, and then, when he saw her panties, his eyes nearly popped out of his head.

"Are those...?"

"They're my panties, Daddy," Esme said with as much dignity as she could muster.

"If I'd have known that this is the kind of underwear hippie chicks wear..."

Esme put her hands on her hips. "Hippie chick?!"

"You do tarot readings and you want to be a professional yoga instructor."

She couldn't help but let a smile play across her face. "And what about this?" She pulled her top up over her head, feeling the fabric graze her already hard nipples as she did so. "Is this the kind of bra a hippie chick would wear?"

"Apparently, yes," Rainer said, his eyes glued to her chest. "Hot damn, Esme, you're gorgeous."

There was that burn in her cheeks again. It was getting to be a very familiar feeling.

"Should I take these off now?"

Rainer leaned against the wall, crossed his arms, and nodded. Why was it that Esme felt as though he was enjoying this?

She unclipped her bra, letting it fall to the floor.

"Darling, remember, we tidy as we go." He pointed to a chair where the rest of her clothes had been folded. Esme made a little indignant noise, then bent down to pick up her bra. She let her ass stick up in the air for a moment longer than she needed to, knowing that Rainer would like the show. Then, she stood up and slipped off her panties, too.

"Daddy can take those for you," he said, holding out his hand, trying his best to sound like someone who hadn't been checking out her butt just now.

There was something so indescribably intimate about handing him her underwear, still warm from her body. He thanked her and put her clothes down on the chair.

"I'm gonna hate this," she said, shivering. Her skin was already puckered with goosebumps and her nipples were hard as rock.

"It'll be over before you know it. Come on, stop putting it off, Little one. And next time you're thinking about breaking Daddy's rules, remember this feeling. Hopefully, it'll put make you think twice."

It's hard to describe why exactly Esme was so scared of the cold. There was something primal and ancient about it. She knew how horrible it would feel, how raw she'd be.

"Come on, come on, come on," she whispered under her breath. "People go through so much worse than this." She stepped over the threshold.

"Ready?" Rainer asked.

She nodded.

Without any more warning or notice, Rainer flipped the faucet next to the shower, and a moment later, a torrent of icy cold water engulfed her.

The instant the water hit it was like she forgot who she was. No past, no future, there was just the cold. It knocked the breath out of her, like all the air in her lungs had been pushed straight out.

"Holy, holy, holy, *shit*!" she screamed, not caring about cussing. There was no way she could stop herself right now. "Oh my god, oh my god, oh my god." She was prancing from foot to foot as her body tingled in the cold. She rubbed her arms, shook her head, breathed deep, did *anything* she could to try to warm up, try to remember that she was alive.

"You're doing great, my little icicle. Not much longer now."

"Arrgghhhh!" She barely recognized the primal sounds she was making. How had early peoples ever managed to survive the freezing cold conditions they'd been exposed to? Never mind that — how did animals like horses manage to just stand in the rain for hours without constantly yelping and screaming?

Then, just when she thought she couldn't take another second, it was over. She was left panting and shivering in the cubicle, but only for a moment, before Rainer stepped in and wrapped her up in the coziest, snuggliest, thickest towel that she'd ever felt.

"D-d-d-daddy," she said, her teeth chattering, "I made it."

"You did," he said, rubbing her body through the towel. She felt her nerves start to tingle as warmth returned to her at his touch. "I'm proud of you. You just did something really hard."

"A cold shower?"

"No. You faced up to a fear."

Well, shoot. She had.

There was an afterglow, a definite afterglow. In the minutes after the cold shower, Esme felt more alive than she had done for a long time. It was like her whole body was more sensitive, more alert than it had been before. And there was a deep but subtle relaxation that took hold of her, too.

"How are you feeling?" Rainer's voice was low and tempting.

"Pretty blissed out," Esme replied. She was lying front-down on Rainer's bed, still naked, her butt and upper legs covered by a thick, soft towel. It was warm in here and she felt delicious.

"So, I take it you'll be making cold showers a regular part of your daily routine?"

"Absolutely not, Daddy." She smiled, then felt a wonderful warm sensation as Rainer dripped body-temperature massage oil onto her upper back.

Esme opened her eyes and saw Om Baby perched on the bedside table. Like her, her stuffie was lying on her front. Like her, her stuffie looked very, very happy.

"You'll always get aftercare after a hard punishment," Rainer said, his hands making a rainbow shape across her upper back. He moved his hands back to the center and repeated the movement.

"Humma humma humma," Esme said, struggling with the intensity of pleasure and relaxation that he was giving her.

"Words, little one."

"I just mean, that's nice."

"This is nothing."

As he drew his hands down her body, she felt like she was melting away. It was like the shower but in reverse. While the cold water had been streaming over her, she'd felt lost in the shock of discomfort. Now, she felt lost in the hug of ecstasy.

He felt so strong. His fingers worked over her soft but firm flesh, squeezing and pounding, rubbing and stretching. She barely even noticed when he subtly, artfully slipped his hands over the top of her buttocks.

She might not have noticed, but her body did.

Waves of pleasure started to radiate out from her center, building and building.

"Daddy," she whispered, her eyes closed.

"I'm so glad you're safe," Rainer said. Esme felt him lean in and kiss her hair. She could feel the heat of his body as he was close to her, and she could smell his musky, clean aroma. "I hated being apart from you, hated not knowing where you were."

"I'm sorry Daddy. I'll never do it again, I promise."

"You need your own space," he said, slipping the towel off her legs and butt. She was briefly aware of the fact that she was totally naked in front of him, but she didn't feel vulnerable. She felt cared for. She felt seen. "And you'll always have that with me. I just want to make sure you're as safe as can be."

His slick, oiled hands dipped down between her legs, smoothly rubbing her inner thighs, making her breath catch in her throat at the unexpected, overwhelming sensation of it.

"I want to be safe, too, Daddy."

"Good girl. Spread those legs for me, sweetheart."

She didn't need to be told twice. The moment she parted her thighs, she felt his fingers trace a line up her dripping wet pussy. It was a shot of pure pleasure, and she felt her brain buzz at the intensity of it.

His fingers moved slowly, perfectly, over her velvet lips. Gently up, firmly down, skillfully, purposefully, avoiding her clit as his other hand squeezed a buttock, intensifying the feeling a hundred-fold.

How was he making her feel this good just with his fingers? It was like he knew exactly what her body wanted, precisely what her body needed.

"Daddy," she moaned, "that feels good."

"You need to know that I'm into you, Esme. I'm into your face. Your lips, your eyes. I'm into your body. Your curves, your bumps, your perfect, perfect ass." He pushed his fingers up into her entrance and she gasped. "And I'm very, very into your pussy."

There was no resisting it, no fighting the sensation as he delved deeper into her. Esme felt herself tensing almost immediately, as the ecstasy started to overwhelm her. She felt Rainer's lips at the nape of her neck, and his fingers started to swirl gently inside her, before — in a moment that took her breath away — his thumb found her clit.

"Ffffuuuuu Daddy..." she groaned, giving up control.

The orgasm was sensational, more powerful than any she'd experienced before, and as her body bucked, it felt like she was sinking deep down into a pit of pleasure that she'd never, ever escape.

CHAPTER THIRTEEN

THERE IS SUCH A thing as a life-changing orgasm. A physical experience so profound and intimate that it reaches deep into your soul and gently unspools you, before reorganizing you into a better, happier shape.

Esme was glowing. She had been this way ever since Rainer's fingers had worked their magic on her. It was impossible to stop thinking about it — the warmth, the power of the cascade of joy he'd sparked in her, it was as if all the crud that had been dammed in her had finally broken out, and peace could flow through her again, unimpeded.

"Morning, smiler," Rainer said. "You look incredible today."

He leaned in and kissed the top of her head, then he found her lips — a long, lingering kiss that left her panting.

"How did you do it?" Esme asked, ignoring his question.

"Do what? The kiss?"

"No, Daddy. How did you do what you did to me last night?"

"Make you feel good?"

"Not just good." Esme was wearing one of Rainer's sweaters this morning. It was so snug and warm that it felt like she was wearing a woolen dress. "You made me come so hard I feel reborn."

Rainer shrugged "I dunno. Just did what felt right."

He came around behind her and embraced her, letting his hands graze her breasts and land on her tummy, before gently rubbing her. "I think sometimes people just fit together."

"Like two pieces of a jigsaw puzzle?"

"Exactly." He started to kiss her neck, leaving her skin tingling. "You and I, we were meant to be. My fingers, your pussy, they were designed for each other." He trailed his hand up her body, making her shiver with anticipation. The memory of what he'd done to her last night loomed over her like a threat — she wanted it again. "Our mouths fit perfectly. Your scent is perfect for me, your voice sounds divine to me. You're my forever girl."

Forever girl.

Esme had never thought she'd meet someone who made her feel like this — who was so perfect it already felt as though he were a part of her.

"How can you be sure?"

"A Daddy knows, sweetheart. I just know."

He moved his hands up, gently cupped her breasts, felt her reactive nipples through the pullover, and Esme gasped as he gently squeezed.

"I want you Daddy," she groaned.

"I know you do, babygirl," he whispered in her ear, squeezing her breasts gently. "But I'm afraid we're gonna have to stick to the schedule."

As he pulled away, Esme cursed the wet lust he'd caused in her pussy, and the fizz she felt in her chest right now. "You're the worst," she sighed.

"I'm the best. Now, drink your smoothie. You've got some yoga to do. Oh, I almost forgot to ask. How would you like to stay up past your bedtime today?"

Her eyes widened with excitement. "Really, Daddy?"

"If you do your chores today — and that includes washing the plates after lunch — then you can. I've got somewhere special to take you."

Oohhh. Somewhere special.

"I'll do all my chores and then some," said Esme, grinning.

It felt so good to be a good girl. Sure, it felt even better to be called a good girl by Daddy, but doing her chores and sticking to her regimen was surprisingly satisfying.

Breakfast. Yoga. Tooth brushing. Drawing. Play time. Lunch.

It was like she was working through a checklist, and each time she finished something it was an accomplishment.

Her yoga was improving. She'd never had a problem with flexibility — she'd been blessed with a naturally flexible physique, and she'd been practicing for years. No, for her, the trouble came with staying with the breath, and being present. Her mind tended to wander, flitting from problem to problem like an anxious butterfly. Anxious breathing always weakened her core.

Today though, the butterfly felt a little more relaxed than normal, and her core felt stronger.

If she wanted to be a good yoga teacher, she needed to connect with that well of inner peace she knew was inside her, and developing a calm practice of her own was crucial for that.

After lunch, she watched a couple of videos about confidence, and made some notes on ideas to help her with her own teaching style.

Esme even managed to avoid touching herself all day long — Daddy was going to be so proud of her. By the time Rainer was due back, she'd almost convinced herself that under the right circumstances, maybe she *could* teach a class. A one-on-one class, maybe, but still it would be something.

"That's amazing," Rainer said, after she'd told him about her day. "You're a superstar." She always loved the way he smelled after working at the garage. It was like he'd sprayed himself with *Essence of Man*. She must have been going crazy to find the smell of gasoline and engine grease to be so good.

"I'm so grateful for your help," Esme said. "Oh, and Om Baby has been doing down dog all day long." She'd gotten into the habit of updating Rainer on her stuffie each day. She liked to shift Om Baby around into a cheeky pose while her Daddy was out so that he was surprised when he got home.

"She'd doing very well," Rainer replied.

"So, so, so, do I deserve to have a super-fun, exciting time tonight?" Esme grabbed Rainer's hand and tugged it gently, trying to get him to agree.

"I think so." He paused for a moment. "Darling, you trust me, don't you?"

Esme felt a pang of nerves. "I do."

"Good. Then let's get ready. We're going out!"

Esme hadn't been out with Rainer before. It felt so good. She knew that it was a little vain and silly, but it was amazing to have such a handsome-looking man on her arm. She still felt as though she didn't deserve to be with him, which is why going out in public made it feel so real.

He was telling the world that he wanted to be with her.

They had dinner at this funky diner-style place in Manhattan. The burgers were thick and the shakes were thicker. The best part of the dinner, though, was seeing Rainer enjoy himself. They were laughing and joking, and everything felt natural.

"Truth is," Rainer said as he finished his burger, "I could study cuisine for literally ten years, cook every day, learn from the best chefs in the universe, and I'd never make something even half as tasty as this simple cheeseburger."

"That was a good one, though," Esme said. "It was like, the Daddy of all cheeseburgers."

"The Daddy, huh?"

"Mmmhmm."

"What am I?"

"You're the Daddy of all Daddies."

Esme felt almost in a daze when they left, like everything in the world was finally going her way.

"Do you miss your streaming?" Rainer asked as they walked down the street. The lights were twinkling, and the feeling of possibility was all around.

"Kinda," Esme admitted. They had their arms linked at the elbow, and she was leaning lightly on her Daddy as he led the way. "I was building a community. I might go back to it at some point, but the stalker guy freaked me out. It's scary to think that he managed to get all my personal information that easily."

Rainer nodded. "Remember, if you want to take it up again, I'll help you keep secure."

"So, where are we going next?" she asked, eager to find out what he had in store for her.

"Actually, we're almost there."

She followed his gaze down the street to a bar. A very strange-looking bar.

"What does that say?" Esme squinted. "Otto's... Shrunken Head?"

"Trust me," Rainer said.

It had been a while since Rainer had felt this far out of his comfort zone. He'd had drinks in plenty of bars around the city, but never once had he visited anywhere quite like Otto's Shrunken Head.

"This place is so cool!" shrieked Esme, as they walked in. The sound of drums pounded from hidden speakers.

"I never really *got* Tiki bars. Is the point that they're meant to be an authentic Hawaiian experience?" He glanced at the rows of cheap, knock-off voodoo paraphernalia on the shelves behind the bar.

"The point is, silly, that they're meant to be fun!"

Esme was in her element. She ordered the biggest, pinkest, flounciest cocktail in the place, and soon, she was bobbing her head along to the music and grinning at the other patrons.

Rainer was waiting for the right time to let her know why exactly they were here.

"Remember, just one drink tonight," he said.

"But, Daddy, this is so tasty. Plus, these cocktails are packed full of fruit."

"The alcohol cancels out any goodness that might be in there, I'm afraid."

"Aww but look!" She picked out a cherry on a stick and held it up to his eyes. "It's packed full of riboflavin."

"Riboflavin, huh?"

"Yes, Daddy," she said in a very serious voice. "Essential for the regulation of the function of the spleen."

Rainer couldn't help but laugh. "Listen, Little one, it's gonna be one drink tonight. It's a school night."

Plus, you're going on stage in a moment.

"Fine," she grumbled. "Although, maybe *this* might be an appropriate time for me to push my limits and see—"

"Just a tip," Rainer interrupted, "don't give away your sneaky plans to Daddy before you act them out."

Her eyes widened. "Ummm, you misheard me. I said something else. Whatever you thought I said, I said the opposite."

"Good." He breathed in deep. "Now, listen, I brought you here for a specific reason." He pointed up at a poster on the wall. It was an advert for the "World-Famous Otto's Shrunken Head Open Mic Night!"

"Wowee! I love shows. Wait..." She looked at him with wonder. "Are you performing for me?"

Rainer grimaced. "Actually, babygirl, I thought *you* might want to."

The color drained out of her cheeks. "Me? Perform?"

"Yeah. That contortionist show you did for me. Or maybe some yoga. I thought you might like to do it here. To be seen." As soon as the words left his mouth, he sensed that he'd got this badly, badly wrong.

Esme was looking around, like a rabbit watching for hawks. "In front of all these people?"

"You don't have to. I just thought... you're never going to see them again. They're strangers and—"

"That's even worse," she hissed. "That's so much worse."

Esme started to wring her hands and tap her feet. He could feel her nervous energy like a physical thing, tugging and pulling at him.

"Babygirl, you're safe. No-one's forcing you to do anything."

"You think I should be able to do it, don't you? You think I'm pathetic if I don't do it."

"No! I don't. It's a big step."

"I should do it." She was looking into the distance and was talking as though possessed. "I'm gonna do it. I'll go and put my name down." It felt like she'd shut down. "Doesn't matter if they all judge me. Doesn't matter if it's a disaster."

"Honey, please, listen to me. Stay centered, breathe. You're *safe*."

At the word safe, she snapped. Her eyes focused on his, and she said, in a voice he almost didn't recognize, "No-one's safe. We could all die, any of us, at any moment."

She stepped away from the table, and for a moment, it looked as though she was heading to the stage. But then, in a moment Rainer would never forget, she let out a huge, terrified, defeated sob, and broke straight for the door.

CHAPTER FOURTEEN

H E'D NEVER MOVED SO fast in his life. Leaving his drinks, his phone, his everything on the table and bolting after the most important thing in the world to him, his Little. He caught Esme outside, stepped in front of her just as she was about to step into the flow of traffic.

A taxi beeped angrily and swerved to avoid them. Esme screamed in fear and stepped back, before falling down on her bottom. It was as though she had suddenly been pulled back into reality. She looked up at Rainer and hugged her knees in close to her chest.

"Daddy," she sobbed, "I'm sorry."

"Darling," he said, full of sadness, "you don't have a thing to apologize for. I'm sorry I put you in that situation. I thought you might find it fun, find it healing..." He sat next to her on the sidewalk. "I made a stupid mistake bringing you here without telling you what I had in mind."

"I just got so scared."

"It's all my fault."

"I'm a failure. I should be able to do it. A normal person, a person who's not a total scaredy-cat, would be able to do it!" There was rage mixed in with her sadness. Rainer felt awful. How could he have done this to the person he cared about most in the whole world?

"You. Are. Not. A. Failure." He locked eyes with Esme as he spoke. He needed her to understand. "Performing for people is very nerve-wracking. I should have known. I should have been more careful. It's nothing like teaching."

"I'm useless. I could never teach anyone anything."

Just then, Rainer had an idea. An idea so perverse and strange that he barely felt brave enough to share it with Esme. An idea that would be embarrassing to him in the extreme.

But surely, Esme was worth it.

"Darling," he said, kissing the top of her head, "everything's gonna be okay. I promise." He breathed in deep. "Now, I've got an idea. It's a dangerous idea, but I think you're gonna like it."

Esme's face brightened, just a little bit. "What is it?"

"Hop on my bike. We're going to your place."

"My place?"

"Yeah. We're gonna need to pick up a spare yoga mat."

A look of confusion appeared on Esme's face.

"How are you at teaching beginners?" Rainer asked.

"I don't know, I mean..." she trailed off as she realized what he was suggesting. "Daddy, are you serious?"

"I'd do anything for you, pumpkin."

Rainer regretted saying that he would do anything for her. After a relaxing night curled up next to his Little, she'd woken him early and revealed her dastardly plan to him. He'd protested, but only for a moment. He could see how much it meant to her.

"I thought yoga was meant to be relaxing!" His voice cracked as he tried desperately to push farther into the pose. The inelegant shape his body was making was very different from the position that Esme had expertly bent herself into.

"Hmmm," Esme said. "I wouldn't say it's relaxing exactly. More like it teaches you to accept pain. Which can be relaxing, in a way!"

They were in downward dog, a position which Esme had described as "Yoga 101," but felt anything but entry-level to Rainer. He had his hands on the ground and was bent at the middle. His butt stuck up in the air, and his feet were planted on the mat. He was, effectively, on his tiptoes, in contrast to Esme, who had her heels nicely grounded.

"You mean to tell me," he grunted, "that all those super-smiley girls in yoga classes are actually in agony?"

"Well, some of the poses can be restorative, but the idea is to push yourself, if only a little."

Rainer tried again to connect his heels to the mat. There was absolutely no chance, zero, of him ever being able to do it.

"Okay, let me take a look." Esme pulled herself out of the pose and walked over to Rainer. "Well, this is definitely a very good effort Daddy. Your legs are almost straight which is good — ah, you're clenching your jaw, try relaxing that."

He did as she asked and instantly felt less tension in his shoulder and arms. "Can't believe that helped."

"Oh yeah, it's all connected. Now, do you mind if I touch you?"

He snorted. "Don't need to ask, sugar."

"Well, in a class I would."

"Right, right, sorry, yep. You have my permission, coach."

Esme made some gentle adjustments to the position of his arms, and she shifted his shoulders back a little. The pose felt a little easier afterward.

"One key thing is that you shouldn't worry about getting the pose exactly like mine," she said. "Everyone's body is different."

"Your body is *very* different to mine."

He heard Esme let out a little chuckle. "Now Daddy, shift forward into a plank pose for me."

Rainer did as she asked, and immediately felt a burn in his abs. He worked out plenty, but there was something about this exercise that made his whole body feel like it was working, all the time.

"Good, very good," now lower down until your chest almost touches the floor, then push up, but keep your... ahem... groin, near the ground."

This felt really good. Almost like a press-up, but the position he ended up in was a relief, after the way his body had been stretching in the downward dog.

"This is an up dog," Esme explained.

Rainer was so happy that he'd managed to cheer her up. Obviously, he'd made her swear that she'd never tell anyone in the MC that he'd agreed to do a yoga class with her, but he hoped that this good decision would make up for the earlier fuck-up. "Everything's some kind of dog?"

"No, silly. Not even close."

The lesson went on for another half an hour or so. Even though it clearly wasn't something Rainer had ever done before, he *could* see the appeal. The feeling after a deep stretch was fantastic, and there were some genuinely challenging strength-focused positions, too.

"Well," he said, at the end of the session, lying on his back, "far as I'm concerned, you're a damn fine teacher."

"Really?"

"Might just be the *shavasana* talking, but I think I might do yoga again sometime."

Even though he had his eyes closed, he felt Esme come and lie down near him. He could sense the heat from her body.

"Do you really mean that? You're not just saying that?"

"Daddies don't lie."

Esme slipped her hand into his and shifted so that she was closer to him. "My lesson made you want to try yoga again. That's... the nicest thing anyone's ever said to me."

"I'm glad."

"Daddy, there's something I want to tell you. I've never told anyone else. Not since it happened."

"You can tell me anything, pumpkin." He rolled over onto his side and looked into beautiful eyes. They were rimmed with tears, and he felt his heart jerk as he felt her pain.

"This is a bad thing."

"I won't judge."

"I can't believe I'm telling you this. It still hurts me when I think about it..." She opened her mouth, then closed it again. "I'm not sure I can do this."

Rainer stroked her hair tenderly. "You can do anything, pumpkin."

Was this the best idea in the world, or the worst? It had to be the best. Being honest with people was always for the best, right? That's what her Daddy said. It was just so painful to go to that place again. She'd spent years trying to forget what had happened to her, and now, she was about to share it with someone who didn't just think she was a freak, or a floaty, flighty, mess.

She hoped it was a good thing to do. Prayed it.

"I used to have a sister. Called Rowan."

Perfect, sweet Rowan. Her clever, funny, wonderful sister. Golden-haired Rowan. Kind Rowan.

"I didn't know."

"She was two years younger than me, and basically my opposite. My parents always used to say I was a nightmare as a baby, that I would kick and scream and barely sleep. Then Rowan came along. She was quiet and kind and slept through the night from basically day one. They loved her. It's not like they were ever mean to me exactly, and I knew that they loved me too, but they *really* loved Rowan."

"That must have been hard for you."

Esme was taken aback by this statement. It was such an obvious thing to say. The kind of thing she would say to someone else if they'd said this to her about a sibling. And yet, no one had ever said it to Esme before. And she'd never thought of it. We rarely consider our childhood when we are children, and Esme hadn't thought that her childhood with Rowan was anything but normal up until this point.

"I guess it was hard for me. I think maybe I was jealous, and then I felt guilty for feeling jealous. Geez, that sounds deep, but I barely thought about it at the time."

"That's normal, I think."

"When we got older, and started going to high school, I used to walk Rowan there. Obviously, we'd walk the same route every day. I remember it clearly. We passed a Jewish bakery that always — always — smelled of chocolate. And there was the laundromat and the pawn shop, plus all our friends' apartment blocks. We lived about twenty minutes from the school, and I was proud that my parents thought I was responsible enough to get my sister there safely. I felt like her guardian." That last word caught in Esme's throat.

Rainer was quiet. Maybe he could already tell where this story was headed.

"There was this intersection my mom always told us to look out for, but I was young and I didn't think there was any chance of an accident." Esme swallowed. "You know what distracted me?"

Rainer gave her a tender, supportive look. "What was it, darling?"

"A boy," she said, sniffing. "From my school. Someone I liked. You know, I never even heard the car hit Rowan." Her voice was wavering, breaking. "First thing I noticed was the crowd. All looking at me like I'd done something terrible. I couldn't work it out, didn't understand, because I was still facing the wrong way. Then I turned." Her voice sounded hollow. "They told me afterward she'd just stepped into the road without looking. The guy who hit her was drunk."

"Oh, babygirl." Rainer put his hand on her knee.

"People were crying, trying to help her. Even the drunk guy, the guy who'd hit her, was out of his car, trying to put right what he'd done. But I was just standing there, not able to move. I was too scared even to look. Everyone was watching me. Everyone knew I was to blame."

"Darling, you weren't to blame."

"That's not what my parents thought." Esme became strangely calm, as though the clarity of the situation had just kicked in. "After the funeral, everything fell apart. My parents *told* me that they still loved me. They *pretended* to comfort me. But every time they thought I was out of earshot, they screamed at each other. About me. About my sister. About the fact they didn't love each other anymore."

"You poor, poor girl."

Esme was sobbing, each word painful for her. "They broke up. They couldn't stay together. How are you meant to stay together when the daughter you hate killed the daughter you love?"

"You know it wasn't your fault."

"It was just fate," Esme sobbed, telling herself the only thing that had kept her sane since the accident. "It was all just fate."

"Esmeralda," Rainer said, "I'm here for you. You just did something very hard, and I want you to know that I'm grateful."

She looked up at her Daddy. She had to look a complete mess right now — tear-stained cheeks and red-rimmed eyes — but he held her gaze. Somehow, she kept looking back at him, daring to believe for just a moment that he didn't think she was a terrible person.

"Now, I'm gonna say something hard. It's not up to me to decide whether or not your sister's death was your fault. By the way, I absolutely think it was *not* your fault. But the only person whose opinion matters is you. You've got to decide."

"It's so hard not to feel guilty."

"It's one of the hardest things in the world. You know, I get why you're so into fate. You *want* your sister's death to have been fate, don't you? Because that means you couldn't do anything to stop it."

Esme nodded. It was a hard truth to admit to, but an obvious one.

"I get it, and I get why you need to believe that. But... truly, I don't think it was fate."

"You mean I could have saved her?" It was agony to face up to this.

Rainer shook his head. "No. The driver was drunk. That was *his* decision to drive drunk. He took control of that situation and put every single person on his route in danger. It wasn't fate – it was caused by a shitty drunk driver. But it wasn't your fault. You were a child."

"You don't hate me?" Esme sniffed.

"Not even close, poppet."

His arms opened wide for her and he took her close, held her against his steel-cut chest, embraced her with warmth and acceptance.

For the first time since the accident, she considered that it hadn't been fate.

And maybe that was okay.

Esme felt overwhelmed — when she thought about everything this man was giving her, it was as though she was lost in a sea of generosity and kindness.

"You make me feel... special," she said, eventually.

"You *are* special," Rainer replied. His face was so close, his lips so tempting, she couldn't help but just reach up...

The kiss was pure passion, an exchange of trust and respect in physical form. The heat of it took Esme by surprise, as Rainer's dominant nature started to show itself. He dictated the pace of the kiss, guiding her with his tongue, showing her how to respond. Everything she did was a mirror of him, was a reaction to his demands and needs. She trusted him. She needed him.

"Daddy," she panted, "I want more. I want it all. Everything."

"Babygirl," he said, his breath heavy too, "do you think you're ready for it? For me?"

"I know I am." Her hand was searching for any tiny scrap of exposed flesh. She wanted to touch him so badly it was like her body was on fire. His skin was so smooth and so warm. She ran fingertips over his inked skin, felt tiny ridges where the ink of his tattoo lay beneath the epidermis.

"You're mine, aren't you?"

"Completely."

Rainer brushed his thumb over her mouth. She kissed it, then slipped the tip between her lips.

"Esme, I've known you were mine for a long time. I've felt it about you."

Esme felt Rainer's hand moving down her back, resting in the small of it, before cupping her butt and gently squeezing.

"You're my forever girl."

He found her lips again, and this time, the intensity and passion were almost overwhelming. All she could do was to give herself to him, let him take what he wanted from her, as her body squirmed in reaction to his touch. She felt his hard cock, straining against her body through their clothes, and she moaned at the thought of what he would feel like inside her.

"I'm going to find your pussy wet, aren't I?"

"Maybe," she winced, biting her lip at the shame of it.

"Daddy can tell." He lifted her skirt and rubbed his thick fingers on her slick panties. She couldn't help it: she yelped with pleasure and humiliation. "Holy cow, Esme, you're wetter than wet."

It was true. Esme had always been quick to arousal, but with Rainer it was a whole new level. Her panties were soaked, and she could feel the moisture on the soft flesh of her inner thighs.

"Ffuuuckkkk," she shuddered.

Instantly, Rainer said, "Good girls don't cuss." He hoisted her up and over his lap.

"Daddy, please, no!"

"I'm afraid so. Not only have you soaked your panties, but you're cussing, too."

His broad hand smacked her tender butt with force, and she shook with pleasure as the pain subsided.

More, Daddy, please, spank me again.

"Daddy, no, I can't take it—"

Another slap, ringing and high-pitched, as Esme lost herself in the sensation again. She could feel his cock so clearly, outlined against her body. If she just wriggled a little to the right....

She got her hand underneath herself and rubbed his hardness.

Rainer moaned with pleasure and annoyance. "How dare you? I'm in charge here, young lady." Without so much as a warning, he lifted her up. "You've earned yourself a serious punishment." His eyes intense, burning into her soul. "I'm gonna fuck you so damn hard that you're gonna come until you pass out."

She felt excitement fill her heart. Finally.

Rainer placed her down on the bed, bent over the side, Esme's butt sticking up in the air, her now-dripping panties still on. She looked over her shoulder, watching as he tugged down his pants.

Well, effing eff.

He was hung like a monster. His cock made other cocks look like toothpicks. This beast of an implement was so thick and deeply veined that it honestly felt as though she had no chance of taking him into her.

"Daddy," she whimpered, "is this gonna hurt?"

"Not even a little bit."

He leaned in close, then he tugged her panties to the side. Just before she felt the hard, warm smoothness of the tip of his shift, she heard him whisper in her ear. "My forever girl. Daddy's gonna take good care of you."

Then, it was there — *he* was there. Resting at her entrance.

"Daddy, I want it. I can't wait any longer. My body is on fire."

"Open up for me."

And he started to slowly, slowly, push her apart. The pleasure center of her brain started to go berserk — she was being stretched so wide and filled so deep that she thought the sensation would snap her in two, and just as the feeling was getting to be so intense that she could barely take it...

Disaster struck.

A knock at the door.

"They'll go away," Rainer hissed.

But they didn't. The knock — heavy and insistent — continued, until finally, words, spoken with a strange urgency.

"Rainer, open up. It's Dog. We need to talk."

CHAPTER FIFTEEN

RAINER WAS NOT READY for what was waiting behind the door. Sure enough, it was Dog, but he looked terrible. There was blood streaming down half his face, and his cut was torn from shoulder to belly. His pants, similarly, were scuffed and shredded, and by the looks of things, there was asphalt embedded in his knee.

"Fuck, Dog!" Rainer cried, lurching forward.

For a moment, it looked as though Dog was about to collapse. He didn't, though. He managed to steady himself before he fell forward.

"I'm alright, I'm fine." Dog sounded hoarse, and almost annoyed by the fuss Rainer was making over him. When Rainer got close enough, it was obvious why. His breath stank of booze.

"What's going on, Dog?"

Somewhere behind him, he heard the muffled gasp of Esme. She must have gotten dressed and seen Dog. For some reason, he felt deeply uncomfortable about Dog seeing Esme here. Not because he was ashamed — it wasn't that at all. It was more because he could now, more than ever before, sense danger coming off Dog like a bad smell.

Luckily, it didn't seem like Dog had noticed her.

"Got into an accident," he slurred, gesturing behind him. There was his hog, twisted out of shape.

So he was drunk-driving. "Fuck. Must have been terrible."

"Didn't feel too good."

"What happened?"

"Fucking pick-up truck. Who needs to drive a fucking pick-up through NYC? Whadda they think they're doing, gonna go wrangle some cattle from the damn ranch in Times Square?"

Rainer took a good look at the hog. "Hit you from the side?"

"Right," Dog said. "Knocked me prone. Bike went over. Hit my head on a fuckin' streetlamp. By the time I was up and shouting, the chickenshit asshole had split."

"You gonna get to a doctor?"

"I'm fine," Dog said. "Just want you to fix up the hog is all."

Rainer's heart dropped. "Might be some time until I can do that."

"Come on, brother, don't hold out on me."

"It's not that. Just got a lot of work on. Struggling to keep up as it is."

He didn't want to be doing this. He wanted to be back in his bed, seeing to that little vixen. The things he would do that that tight, perfect little pussy. It had felt so damn good when even the slightest tip of his cock had edged its way between those velvet lips.

"Hello? Earth to Rainer?"

"Sorry. Zoned out."

"I'm standing in front of you with a head wound and thousands of dollars' worth of business and you... zoned out?"

"Like I said, got a lot on my mind at the moment. Look, I don't want to turn you away. Just got a lot of work on. You'd be better off finding another shop that could turn her around faster."

"I don't care about speed," Dog said, lighting up a cigarette. "I want quality. You're the best."

"Dog, would you mind not smoking?"

Dog looked as though Rainer had just asked him to stand on one foot and dance around in circles.

"What? Why?"

Ugh. He didn't want to say it. "Got company."

It was at that moment that Esme decided to join them. "Oh, Dog, you look awful." She was wearing her yoga kit, as well as a short jacket.

"Now there's a confidence booster if ever I heard one."

"Sorry," Esme said. "Are you hurt?"

Esme was being very brave by coming out to talk to Dog, Rainer noticed. She hadn't been too happy about what Dog had said about Littles attending official club meetings. Rainer had thought a lot about the rule. He could totally understand why other MCs had to have member-exclusive meetings. But when Littles were involved, it would be irresponsible to ban them from attending.

"Not too bad thanks, Little one." There was something forced about the way he said that, almost as if the phrase 'Little one' got stuck in his throat. "Didn't know you two were so serious." Dog raised an eyebrow.

"She's mine," Rainer said, not hesitating for an instant. He saw Esme's cheeks change to a bright shade of pink and for a moment he regretted saying it. He hoped he hadn't embarrassed her too much. "And I'm hers. I'd destroy anyone who got in the way of what we have." The strength of conviction surprised him, but he couldn't stop himself.

"Happy for you," said Dog. It was a smile, but there was more than pure happiness behind it. "So, is your Little one heading out?"

"Daddy, are you going to be a while with Mister Dog?"

"Probably," Rainer admitted. He at least wanted to talk Dog through the issues his bike had, and — hopefully — convince him to take it to another garage. Maybe giving him a lecture about drunk-driving while he was at it.

"Okay, um I think in that case I better get going. I kinda forgot all about it because—" more, intense blushing, "— um, I thought I'd be at my place this morning, but I have a yoga class. It's a special one! I can't miss it!"

"More yoga?" It was Rainer's turn for his cheeks to burn. Hopefully, Esme would keep their little secret to herself.

"Mmhmm. No such thing as too much yoga."

Fuck. He was gonna miss her. But it was fair enough that she was leaving. He'd been the one to change the plan.

"Alright, sugarplum. You make sure to text me when you get there safe, though."

"Of course, Daddy. I'm a good girl." She shot Dog a quick look and then leaned in to give Rainer a kiss goodbye. He felt her lips on his cheek, had just enough time to be reminded of her scent, and then, just as she was turning away, she whispered in his ear, in the quietest whisper he'd ever heard, "I'll be thinking about your cock all day."

Rainer tried not to look surprised and tried even harder not to look aroused.

"Alright, *good girl*. I'll see you later."

He stared at her ass unapologetically as she walked away.

"Right," Rainer declared when she was gone, "let's take a look at this poor hog."

The bike talk didn't last too long in the end. The hog was a mess. Fixing it was going to be expensive and time-consuming. Plus, Rainer didn't have the correct parts for it in his garage, so would need to order them in.

"And that's why," Rainer said, after explaining how long it might take him to fix the bike, "you're better off using another place."

Dog shook his head. "Buddy, you're the only guy in town I trust. I'll wait. Keep the bike here until you're ready to work on it. I'll pay you fifty dollars a week just to store the damn thing for me. Then, when you get the time, fix her up. I've got a couple of spares. This one's just my favorite."

Rainer could see why. Harley Davidson did still occasionally make bikes like this, although they tended toward the sleeker, blacker, more intimidating bike styles. This was a 1971 Electra Glide — a shocking blue color, and handsome as Brad Pitt. It was painful to Rainer to see it in this state.

"Honestly, I c—"

"A hundred, then,"

Was he really going to turn down a hundred bucks a week to do nothing?

Rainer let out a deep sigh. "Fine. I'll do the job. I just hate letting people down."

"I know. That's why you'd make a great MC Prez."

This took Rainer by surprise. "You think so?"

"Sure. But I don't stop until I get my way. That's why I'd make an even better one."

It was hot in the studio. Not just a little warm, not even slightly uncomfortably hot. No, this room was sweltering.

At the front, Kelly was pulling a textbook *malasana* — a deep, yogic squat in which her bottom almost kissed the ground. Even she — as perfect as she was in every way — was sweating, her beautiful blond hair stuck in strands to her smooth forehead.

All the other students in the class were suffering, too. Esme heard groans and moans of discomfort as they struggled against the scorching conditions. Each time Kelly adopted a new pose, there was a ripple of irritated effort as the students copied her.

Esme was loving the experience.

Kelly had booked this studio space months ago and had been planning this special hot yoga lesson ever since. The space was above a busy street in downtown Manhattan, and the view from the full-length windows was spectacular — it almost felt as though you were going to tumble forward out of them. Cars and people scuttled by hundreds of meters below, tiny beings on their way to find coffee, love, happiness.

Esme was on cloud nine.

Every single muscle burned with the effort of it. Her skin glowed with moisture as her body tried to keep cool.

Inside, though, she was even hotter than the room. Fizzing with excitement.

As she watched Kelly expertly lead the class, she remembered that just a little while ago, *she* had led a yoga class of her own. Admittedly, she'd had just one student, and he hadn't been the biggest yoga fan in the world, but she had done it. And he'd enjoyed it.

Not only had she taught the lesson, she'd told Rainer her deepest, most shameful, most painful memory. And he'd been wonderful about it.

For the first time in ages, she felt ready for anything. If, right now, Kelly hurt herself and needed someone to finish the class, Esme felt confident she could do it. She'd get right up there and kick these students' asses.

Maybe not literally. That might get her arrested.

"Everyone, back to chair pose."

The class collectively croaked their way into the punishing half-squat. Esme felt her glutes start to quiver and burn with the effort.

Maybe it *was* her fate to lead a yoga class, after all.

Fate.

That was something she hadn't thought about in a while. She normally started each week with a tarot draw for herself. But she hadn't been doing that. Not since she'd been with Rainer. She just hadn't felt like she needed to.

It meant that recently, she had been disconnected from fate. She had no idea what the future held. It was a little bit scary.

"Now, arms up! Reach for the sun!" Kelly commanded.

As Esme brought her fingertips high up above her, she imagined the warmth of the sun, making her glow even more.

Sometimes, it was okay to be scared. It reminded you that you were alive.

Just like Rainer had reminded her this morning.

Oops. That was a dangerous thought. Now, as she brought her palms to heart-center and gazed out of the window ahead, all she could do was imagine him, his cock urgently resting at her entrance and then — without even pulling her panties down — thrusting slowly into her. The sensation had been electric.

Don't get wet, don't get wet!

She couldn't afford to, not in this outfit.

It was as she lay on the floor in a final *shavasana* that a dirty, naughty thought popped into her mind. Maybe she'd come up with an appropriate way to break the rules. Something to make her Daddy punish her, but not get *too* angry...

CHAPTER SIXTEEN

WELL. DOG'S BIKE WAS in his house. His own pickup was at the garage, so Rainer would have to head back there to transport the hog away. Obviously, he could chain it up outside, but he'd worry that opportunistic thieves would pick the loose parts off for scrap money, which would end up costing Dog even more money, and Rainer didn't want that.

So, he'd left it in the widest corridor, which just so happened to be by his front door.

"Why am I even helping the guy?" he asked himself, as he thumbed through a professional parts and services directory he kept at home. "He'd been drinking. He's a mess."

In a way, Dog was his enemy. His rival. They were both aiming to be Prez of the club, for very different reasons. Still, it never really felt as though Dog was upset with him or bore him any animosity. So, it was hard to feel anything bad about the guy.

Mainly, he was annoyed with Dog for scaring Esme away.

He'd been so close. So *fucking* close to fucking.

The thought of it — of her — was driving him mad. Maybe he should just head into the bathroom and jerk one out, so that he could calm down and finally think about something else. Trouble was, Rainer knew that the only thing that could stop the burning in his loins was Esme, and lots of her.

Luckily, he didn't have too long to wait.

She sent him a message to say she was on her way back like the good girl she was, and it wasn't so much longer before she knocked on the door, her tiny hands making a much different sound to the pounding, desperate thumps of Dog a few hours ago.

"Who could that be?"

"A Little friend."

He swung open the door and there she was, in all her sweaty, perfection.

Hang on. Wait a minute.

"Babygirl," he said suspiciously, "I was all ready to welcome you back with open arms, but I need to ask you a very serious question."

"Oh no! Have I done something wrong?"

"That remains to be seen." He crossed his arms. "You remember our rules, right?"

"Mmhmm. I think so."

"Remember the one about showering after exercise?"

It was so difficult to read the look on Esme's face. Was she surprised and shocked? Was she embarrassed because she was caught in a deliberate act? Or was she — most likely — relishing the uncertainty she was causing?

"Ohhhhhh yeah..." she said, biting her lip. "I do remember that rule. What a sensible rule, Daddy."

"Right. So tell me, did you sh—"

Esme was already shaking her head. "Little Esme forgot! I was too excited to get back home to you! I didn't want to be late back."

Rainer shook his head. "Oh dear. This is very serious. Very serious."

"It is?"

"Come with me."

"B-but, b-bubububububut, what if I *die*?!"

Rainer let out a deep, resonant chuckle. "At least it's a cool way to go out."

Esme looked at the bath-tub full of freezing cold water and fought hard against the urge to laugh at her Daddy's dumb pun. Finally, she managed it, keeping her lip curled into a scowl of indignation.

"Not funny!" she yelped and batted him on his intimidatingly huge shoulder. "If I *do* pass away, can you put something witty on my gravestone?"

"Here lies Esmeralda... um... survived by her stuffie Om Baby and her very handsome Daddy, who's also a great budding chef?"

"I said witty, not annoying."

"Now, now, Little one. I think it's about time for those sweaty workout clothes to come off, don't you?"

"A cold shower is one thing, but a cold bath is just... evil."

"Breaking the rules is not something you want to be doing, Little one." And then, he added, quietly, "Especially on purpose."

Should she pretend? Should she kick and scream and fight like hell to make him think it had been an accident?

No. She couldn't lie to Daddy. Not really.

"How did you know?"

"Aha! I knew it!"

"You didn't know?" her mouth opened into a wide 'o.'

"I had my suspicions. And I'm grateful to you for coming clean. So to speak."

"So grateful that you're going to change your mind and put some warm water in the tub?" She batted her eyelids at him like a manic cow.

"Nice try, princess. Now, take off those clothes before I take 'em off for you. I suppose the other option is for me to dunk you in the tub fully cl—"

"I'm doing it, I'm doing it."

Of course, it took her quite a while longer to undress than it normally would, but Rainer was surprisingly patient. He seemed to enjoy watching the show.

"You know," he said as she finally undid her bra and let it fall onto the clothes heap she'd been slowly building, "I probably shouldn't say this, but... I love the smell of your sweat."

"Excuse me?"

"It's true." He stepped closer, a hungry look in his eye. "I dunno if there's something wrong with me, or if it's your pheromones or whatever, but..." He gave her skin a long, careful sniff. The intensity of his gaze grew. "It's like fucking catnip for me." Then, to her shock, he lifted her arm and took a deep breath in. "God damn, I swear women aren't supposed to smell this good."

"Daddy, there's something wrong with you."

"It's you, Esme. It's like you were *built* for me. It's like someone took an order without my knowledge and hand-crafted a custom-built, premium-quality *mate* for me. You make me so damn hard, all the fucking time."

She could see the lump at his groin growing again, and shuddered at the thought of the size of him, beneath his pants.

"Daddy, I'm getting wet."

"I know you are." He looked straight at the bath.

"Now?"

"Get in, Little girl, or Daddy's going to be very disappointed."

Esme's heart pounded. She gripped the rim of the bathtub and paused for a moment. "Daddy, it will be alright, won't it?"

"I promise. Look, I even put the towel on the radiator for you. You'll be just fine. Try to enjoy it."

Enjoy it. Well. That was easier said than done. Esme thought about the best way to tackle this. Should she put her feet in one by one, acclimate to the cold and then slowly lower her full body in when she was used to it?

That was probably the way that the *old* Esme would have done things. The Esme that just let things happen to her. Well, that Esme was gone. New Esme took charge of the situation. New Esme kicked fate's ass. New Esme decided just to jump into the fucking tub.

Twenty minutes later, Esme's teeth were still chattering. "D-daddy, I think I might be cold for the rest of my life."

Rainer had had a permanent grin on his face ever since 'the incident.'

"Just remind me," he said, clearly trying not to laugh, "what it was exactly that you said when you splashed into the bath like a kid doing the cannonball at a birthday party."

Esme mumbled under her breath.

"S'cuse me?"

"I said: 'Motherfucking nut-sucking ice-ball cock-freezer.'"

His laugh was ridiculously loud. "Glad you managed to say that without your teeth chattering. Hoo-boy, I'm never gonna let you live that down. With a mouth like that, *you* should be the biker, not me."

"You don't know what it was like, Daddy."

"Cold?"

"Well yes, but it was like... my bones were cold. All the way to the core. It was horrible."

He passed her the hot cocoa he'd been preparing for her. "Hopefully this will help you warm up a bit."

"Thanks, Daddy." She took a sip. It was velvety smooth, super-creamy, with a powerful chocolate punch. The drink was sweet, but only subtly. It was perfect. "Why does this taste so good?"

"Made with love. It's the best taste in the world." He gave her a kiss on her forehead. "Let me know when you're warm, because there's something else we need to do."

"Something else?"

"Yeah. You need to be punished for cussing."

Her jaw dropped. "Daddy, really?"

"Don't worry," he said, with a wicked grin on his face. "This is a punishment you're gonna enjoy. I guarantee."

It was the most beautiful sight he'd ever seen in his life. Esme's naked body, bent over and strapped in place so that she was in a permanent puppy pose.

Her smooth ass stuck up in the air, and her face was down on the ground, resting on a thin pillow he'd provided for her comfort. A position like this wouldn't work for someone who wasn't already flexible — it would be too intense. But for Esme, it was just fine.

"Does that feel comfortable," he asked, seriously.

"Mmmhmm," she said, around the ball gag he'd pushed into her mouth just moments ago.

"Good. Remember, you need to use your safeword, just tap on the floor twice."

"Mmm," she moaned again, saliva dripping around the gag, and pooling on the pillow. Oh, his babygirl was suffering. But in a moment, he was gonna take her to paradise.

"We were disturbed before," he said, taking his time to survey the mound of flesh which lay in front of him. "But that won't happen again. Doesn't matter who knocks at the door, I'm not leaving this room until I've filled that pussy with come."

Esme moaned again. Her pussy was glistening like a jewel between her buttocks. He couldn't wait to feel it around his cock again, couldn't wait to taste her divine flavor.

"Before I fuck you," he continued, "I *am* gonna have to spank you. All that cussing left my hands feeling very twitchy." He kept his eyes on her pussy, and could have sworn that it throbbed as he said the word spank.

Rainer didn't have a huge amount of sex play stuff, but he did always keep a riding crop handy. He found the sound the crop made to be extremely sexy, and the pretty red lines it left were hard to beat.

He took the triangular tip of the crop and ran it gently up Esme's inner thigh. She shivered with pleasure. Before they'd begun this scene, he'd told her exactly what was going to happen. You don't just surprise someone with a riding crop. It was such a specific kind of pain and it could be scary if a sub wasn't adequately prepared.

Rainer ran the crop down her other thigh. The temptation to sink his cock into her was strong. But he wanted to hold back. He knew it would be better for them both to delay the pleasure for as long as he could. This was their first time — their real first time. Had to be something to remember.

"When I strike you with this crop, it's to remind you that Daddy is in control. Daddy sets the rules. Daddy decides when they've been broken."

He knew that he was being extremely strict about the cussing — he'd laughed about it, after all. Plus, he'd been cussing in front of her by mistake lately. Too hard not to when there was so much to cuss about.

But he knew that Esme was *absolutely* getting off on this. It was more of a *funishment* than a punishment.

He brought the length of the crop to rest over both her buttocks. "Ready?"

She moaned.

Rainer dealt out five perfectly aimed strikes with the crop. After each strike, juice spilled from Esme's pussy, and a fiery red line formed on her alabaster buttocks. It was beautiful — she looked like a work of art. Having a Little this flexible made him want to get into rope bondage. He bet that he could make some delicious shapes from her.

As her pleasure grew, so did his arousal. His cock was so hard he had to take off his pants and underwear — it was a physical necessity. There was something primal about dominating a woman like this, mastering her, both of them naked, his cock hard and her pussy wet.

"Well done," he panted, after he finished the five strikes. "You coped with that very well, beautiful."

And as Esme moaned again, he pushed the tip of his cock into her perfect pussy. Her voice hitched, and he felt her body relax with pleasure around him.

How did it feel to be entered by Rainer?

Like medicine for her soul. That's how.

He took her by surprise. No warning, no words, just the inarguable girth of his manhood, spreading her hot pussy wide and filling her up entirely. Of course, that's what they'd discussed before the scene — it's what she had agreed to, what she wanted. But it felt fresh, new, shocking, because she was still lost in the agony and ecstasy of what she'd just experienced.

"Daddy," she tried to moan through the ball gag.

He pushed in deeper, hitting a spot in her that no man had ever reached before. His hands gripped her buttocks, spread them gently apart, and he somehow dove deeper still. Her eyes widened and her body tensed as the truth of his size finally dawned on her. It was a feeling like no other. Her pussy lips stretched deliciously, all of her body full of Daddy's cock.

"That's it, take it for me, take it for Daddy."

She moaned in the affirmative. It felt so good to be held down like this. She couldn't escape the pleasure even if she wanted to. Her whole body felt so sensitive, maybe because of the cold shower or the cropping — perhaps both — that every single one of his touches was making her quiver and shake with pleasure.

"I own you now, Esme, you understand?" He started to slip and slide in and out of her. His cock was slick with her juice and he worked it expertly. He was relentless and slow, like an engine on a low setting, pounding her hard but with restraint. She could feel the power of his body behind his thrusts, and she could feel how much faster and harder he could be doing this if he wanted to. "I'm a possessive man," he said, squeezing her buttocks so hard it felt like he was going to leave handprints on them, "I want everyone to know you belong to me, and no-one else. In fact..." He pulled out of her, and came around to her face, before unclipping the gag and pulling it from her mouth. "I want to hear you say it."

"Daddy, please, fuck me more."

"No cussing!"

He returned to the back of her, and without so much as a warning, he spanked her ass, hard. She felt the sting deep in her core, and then — moments later — in her pussy.

"Sorry Daddy, I just need you so bad."

She didn't have long to wait — his cock was there again, nudging her entrance. It was agony to be teased be him — so, so hard to know that he was in complete control of the situation.

"Say that you're mine," he commanded.

"I'm yours."

His cock started to slip in, then he paused. "I own you."

"You own me."

An inch or two more. She gasped at the sensation of it. "Body and soul."

"*Heart*, body and soul."

"Ohh, I like that. There's the good girl I'm falling for."

And he was in her again. But this time, there was no holding back. Rainer took hold of her hips and moved her as he thrusted. Soon, he was fucking her hard and fast and rough and deep and she couldn't think of anything but the way he was making her feel. She couldn't move, she couldn't think, all she could do was be.

Then, for the first time in her life, she sensed something. She was about to come, and he wasn't even touching her clit.

The sensation was like an eruption. She could feel it building, growing, trembling beneath the earth. "Daddy, I'm close, I'm so close," but by the time she'd finished her sentence, it was there, like a glowing ball of plasma, fully set to engulf and destroy her.

As the waves hit, her body jerked against her bounds. Her eyes throbbed, her brain broke, and it was like she just gave up on anything that wasn't coming. "Ffffuuuuu...dge," she somehow said.

Then, Rainer said something that brought her right back. "Esme, I love you." Then, he pushed his thick cock into her wet, hot, post-orgasmic pussy, and he filled her with his come.

CHAPTER SEVENTEEN

O VER BREAKFAST, THEY GRINNED like Cheshire cats. They flirted like drunks. They giggled like schoolgirls.

There was magic in the air, and both of them could feel it. Rainer fed Esme a spoonful of cereal, and Esme poured cream into Daddy's coffee like a good girl. Om Baby sat nearby, her presence a reminder of their acceptance of each other.

He loved her. He'd said it. Hadn't even thought about it. He meant it more than anything he'd ever said in his whole damn life.

Later in bed together, after he'd read her a story and she'd kissed him about a million times, she'd pulled him in close and said, "Om Baby says that she loves you too, Daddy." He thought it had been fitting she'd used Om Baby to tell him her feelings again.

In Rainer's dreams, they'd be spending the whole day together, taking a day off yoga and work and just about everything but each other. Bad sadly, that couldn't happen.

Today was the day of the election. In just a few hours, the future of the Drifters MC would be decided. Rainer would have to head to the Den. As per Dog's request, Littles weren't allowed at the bar today.

There had been some consternation and argument about that, but in the end, Rainer had relented.

As to the question of becoming President of the club, Rainer wasn't sure how he felt about it. He hoped that he would win — he thought. Part of him worried that he should be more anxious about the vote. But another, bigger part of him knew that — in a way — it was a good sign that he didn't mind so much.

He remembered something his dad had told him about politics when he was growing up: "Anyone who wants to be in charge should be banned from being in charge." At the time, he hadn't really understood what his old man had meant. But now he was older, he got it. A personality that's drawn to power is necessarily dangerous.

"Daddy? You okay? You've gone quiet."

Esme had been coloring a picture of a motorcycle that Rainer had printed out for her. He'd been watching, cooing at how careful she was being, letting her know how clever she was to be staying in the lines so well.

"I'm alright. Just thinking about the election."

"It's a big day, huh?"

"I guess so. Truth is... I don't know what the right thing for the club is."

"It's you!"

"You sure?"

"Mmhmm," she said, sticking her tongue out in concentration as she filled in the front fork. "You're the cleverest, bestest Daddy ever."

"I'm thinking I haven't done enough to show the others that."

"Everyone knows it."

She was so sweet. He got the impression that she really believed it, too.

"You always help people. You'll work on anyone's bike. When there's trouble, you're the first to say you'll deal with it. You never make a fuss. And you don't even mind when people vomit all over your favorite t-shirt."

She looked up at him with those big green eyes. She was his. He could scarcely believe it.

"When I joined the MC, I swore an oath. That nothing would come before the club, before my brothers. But you know, Esme, you're the most important thing in my life. More important than anything else. If you were in trouble, if you needed me, I'd drop everything and come to you. The club doesn't even come close."

"I don't deserve you." She let her head rest on Rainer's arm.

"You do. You deserve so much better than me."

"Can I ask you something, Daddy?"

"Anything."

"Remember when I did that tarot reading for you? You got mad. Told me to leave."

"Mmmhmm."

"Sometimes I get scared and think that something like that might happen again. That you might just kick me out. You might change your mind about me."

Rainer nodded. He knew this would come up sooner or later. In truth, he was happy she'd felt comfortable enough to bring it up at all. "I understand, sweetheart. I hurt you that day. It must be hard to trust me."

"Not exactly. I trust you completely. Just, hard not to feel like I'm holding back a bit, waiting for something bad to happen."

"Babygirl, I'm gonna tell you what happened to me. Why I got so angry that time. Trust is key. That's what it all comes down to."

"I'm listening, Papa Bear."

Papa Bear. He liked that.

"I was just a kid. Growing up rough. My father was a Mexican immigrant who set up his own garage. Struggled for customers and got shook down by the local mob for protection money. We never had much. Felt like we never had anything. Except for my mother, who had plenty. Of trouble, that is. Me and my two brothers – all little assholes. Let's just say I didn't get much hands-on parenting." When he thought back to that time, he found it hard to believe that his mama even managed to get food on the table for them. "I always admired my dad. Saw how hard he worked. He never spent a penny on himself. I grew up in that garage, learning from him, helping him with all the shitty jobs."

"I can imagine little Rainer, covered in grease," Esme said. "It's a cute image."

"Yeah, well I wasn't a cute kid, I promise you. Anyway, when my Papa passed, he left the garage to me and Tuco, my older brother. Carlos, our younger brother, had smarts, and was at a community college studying medicine. Tuco was always fun, but had a crazy, dangerous streak. He always wanted to push things further, sail close to the wind. Anyway, we went into business together. Took over Papa's garage."

Rainer could feel his anger bubbling up inside him, acrid and hot. He took a moment, tried to center himself.

"Trouble was, Tuco was a snake. One day, the cops came knocking at the door. They had a warrant. Searched the place. Course, I didn't know what the problem was, couldn't think why they would be there."

Esme looked shocked. "What had he done?"

"At first, they didn't find anything. But then, they took apart some of the bikes we were working on. And they found bricks of cocaine *inside* the fucking engines."

"Cocaine?"

"I was arrested straight away. Turns out, honest business wasn't enough for Tuco. Instead of pay the mob's protection money, he'd become a drug mule for them. But that's not the way the courts saw it."

"What happened?"

"*I* was sent to prison. I was only twenty-one. Barely old enough to fucking drink." Rainer's face hardened. "Can you imagine it? My brother, lying on the stand to protect himself? Saying that all of it was my fault? My lawyer was blindsided. It was only after seven years in prison that the appeal was upheld. Now, my brother's locked away instead. But he took seven damn years of my life."

"Oh, my goodness. Daddy, I'm so sorry."

"It's okay, sweetheart. It's just... trust don't come easy for me. Not after what Tuco did. And forgiveness comes even harder. So, when you read me those cards..."

"I understand." Esme paused for a moment, looked as though she was trying to decide whether to speak. Then, eventually, she said, "But you know, the cards were right. Those are the issues you're going to have to deal with if you wanna be Prez."

"You're right."

Rainer leaned in and kissed the top of her head.

There was a knock at the door. "Aha," Rainer said. "Your playmate is here."

He went and answered it with Esme. She held his hand the whole way. It felt wonderful to hold her little hand in his.

"Sophia, so good to see you!"

The two girls squealed and embraced each other. Sophia had brought a huge suitcase full of antique stuffies which were in various stages of repair.

"This one needs really specific glass eyes that I had to import from England! And, and, and, this one is German. I call him Der Uberbear!"

It was great to hear them playing together. Om Baby joined in the fun, too, teaching the stiff old bears how to loosen their joints.

"Right, guys," Rainer said after watching them play for twenty minutes or so. "I'm heading to the meeting. Look after each other. I left food in the fridge. Esme, don't just gorge yourself on snacks, okay? Eat the casserole."

"Got it. Snacks only."

Rainer gave her a look.

"I'm joking, Daddy. We'll be very, very good girls, won't we Soph?"

"Sorry, just thinking about making popcorn," Sophia said, grinning.

"You're both impossible," Rainer said. Then he blew his Little a kiss and stepped into the future.

CHAPTER EIGHTEEN

THERE WAS NO MUSIC at the Den today. It was far too serious for that. The candidates had a five-minute window — a last-ditch effort to win the hearts and the minds of the club members before the votes would be cast.

Tatiana, who had become more and more involved in the running of the club since Marcus' passing, had been busy setting up a ballot box and private voting booths. Now, everything was ready to go.

"This is a big day," Tatiana said. She was holding court at the front of the room, eyes scanning the collection of club members who'd come to be part of such a huge moment. "The day we decide on the soul of the club. We have two candidates for presidency. Dog and Rainer. Each different but each dedicated to the MC, in their own way. First up, Dog's going to speak for a few minutes, and he'll be followed up by Mr. Ortiz."

Rainer was interested in what Dog was going to say about the election. He hadn't heard anything from his opponent since he'd dropped his bike around to his apartment. No doubt he'd been canvassing the other members, working overtime to ensure he got the votes he needed. It was going to be an interesting contest.

Dog stood up and headed to the front. There was a grim, determined look on his face.

"Gentlemen," he began. He was looking a hell of a lot better than he had the other day. There was no bruising on his face at all, and no evidence of the wound that had caused so much bleeding. Damn, he'd healed up perfectly. "I stand in front of you today as the only qualified candidate for the presidency of our club."

There was a murmur of disapproval from the club members. Saying Rainer wasn't qualified was a direct insult.

"What does that mean?" Baron asked. He was always swift to stick up for Rainer.

"We all remember our oaths, don't we?" There was a definite swagger to the way Dog was speaking. He was acting like it was in the bag. "We took them after the hazing, after our trial periods as prospects. I remember mine as clear as it were yesterday." He began to recite, and as he did, the whole room began to join in. "I will uphold the rules of the MC. I will aid my brothers whenever they need me. I will obey the command of the club President. Everything else comes second to the club." Then, he repeated, "Everything else comes second to the club."

He let those words ring around the Den. Then, a moment later, Dog said, "Jackie, roll the tape."

A biker with long black hair pressed a button on his phone, and a moment later, a recording started playing over the club speakers.

It took Rainer a moment to realize that it was *his* voice.

"*When I joined the MC, I swore an oath. That nothing would come before the club, before my brothers. But you know, Esme, you're the most important thing in my life. More important than anything else. If you were in trouble, if you needed me, I'd drop everything and come to you. The club doesn't even come close.*"

As the message played out, the eyes of the other club members fixed on Rainer. He didn't even have to think about *how* this had happened. Obviously, Dog had put a bug inside the hog he'd tricked Rainer into taking possession of. It was obvious now — the whole thing had been a ruse. There had been no accident, no injury. Only foul play.

How could Rainer have been so stupid? How could he have let himself trust a snake like Dog? Maybe it was just his fucking destiny.

"Brothers," Dog said, "I put it to you that I'm the only qualified candidate. The only non-oath-breaker." He didn't say another word, he just sat back down.

A murmur of uncertainty echoed around the bar, as the members of the club tried to process what was happening. Rainer's head was spinning. What could he possibly say to persuade the Drifters?

He rose, slowly, then took his place in the middle of the room. For some reason, all he could think about was Esme. She felt suddenly so far away from him, so vulnerable.

"Brothers," Rainer said. "I said those words. You know I'm an honest man. You know that I would never spy on a potential rival or use trickery to further my own ends." Dog shifted uncomfortably in his seat. "But honestly, I don't blame Dog. He wants to be Prez. I never wanted that. You know me. It would be pointless to pretend otherwise."

More murmured conversation from the room. Maybe everyone thought that he was throwing in the towel.

"I don't want to be President. I want the club to decide our future together. As one. I'm not standing here because I think I know best. Or because I have some grand vision for the future of the club." He drew in a deep, deep breath. He was about to stray into some very dangerous waters, but he knew that he had to go there, for the good of the club. "I'm here because I *know* that Dog is the wrong person to lead us."

Dog shook his head and tutted.

"Honestly," Rainer continued, "I think it was a mistake to let him back into the club at all. We're talking about a guy who left. Who dropped his cut on the ground and walked out when we needed him the most. We're talking about a guy who defied Marcus, who insulted him."

Rainer could hear mutterings of agreement from around the room. He had to keep going. He knew it.

"But leave all that aside. Let's forget about his disrespect, his disloyalty. Let's focus on what he's talking about for the future of the club. He wants guns. He wants drugs. He wants power. If he gets his way, there will be no Littles in the Den. Fuck, there would probably be no Littles, period. I get it. This ain't a normal MC. But then if it was a normal MC, we wouldn't all be members, right?"

A more full-blooded wave of agreement came back to him this time.

"Now, I don't know what the club's gonna choose to do if I become Prez, but I've got a feeling that we're not gonna be needing guns. We're not gonna be dealing drugs. And we're not going to be getting into prostitution. If I'm made Prez, I'll be doing everything to get back to the soul of the club: riding hogs and protecting Littles."

There was — to Rainer's surprise — a resounding cheer from the room. Thank goodness for the men of the Drifters. They were good people, not criminals. That's where the heart of the MC lay.

"You know, I think Dog wants me to stand up here and lie. He wants me to say: the Drifters is more important to me than my Little will ever be. He wants me to say: I'd betray Esme for the good of the club. But I won't do it. Because for me, being a Drifter is about being committed to your Little, to *all* Littles. And that's what I am. I'm a Drifter."

This time, people were up on their feet, stamping and clapping, whooping and hollering. Dog, on the other hand, was looking down at his phone, a look of strange calm on his face.

"My belly feels like a popcorn machine." Esme lay on the couch, with one hand on her tummy, groaning as her gut gurgled and bubbled.

"My belly feels like a casserole pot," Sophia replied.

"We ate too much."

"We're the worst."

"Look at Om Baby," Esme grunted. "She's so perfect. So slim and limber, no matter how much food she eats."

"Stuffies have a rough deal, though," Sophia said. "No tastebuds. And also, they've got no bottoms, which makes things uncomfortable."

"Ewwwww!" Esme said, giggling away despite herself.

"It's true. Us stuffie-makers never stitch on butts. Or front butts."

Her Daddy had been away for a couple hours. She'd received a message from him to say that he won the vote. She was super happy for him and was planning a big surprise for when he got back, but she understood that he was going to be out for a while. He needed space to celebrate and just be with the guys, just like she needed space to be Little with friends from time to time.

"Hey," Sophia said. "You're thinking about your Daddy, aren't you?"

"I'm just... so proud of him."

Sophia gave her a sweet smile. "You're a real cute pudding, you know that? When we first met, I was kinda intimidated by you."

"You weren't!"

"Uh-huh. You seemed so spiritual and cool and in touch with all this funky, witchy stuff."

"Now you just see me for the dweeb I am?"

"No, silly! You're still way too cool for me. But it's been nice to get to know the *real* you, too. The vulnerable you."

Vulnerable. It was true. She was vulnerable. But maybe she was vulnerable for the right reasons. Maybe she wasn't ready to be taken advantage of, maybe she'd just opened herself up to love, and to success. And that needed vulnerability.

Just then, Esme's phone chimed. She picked it up and checked it. Hmm, a voice message. She clicked play, and her Daddy's voice rung out.

"The Drifters is more important to me than my Little will ever be."

She played it again, trying to convince herself it wasn't real. Then, a moment later, another message came through. Another recording.

"I'd betray Esme for the good of the club."

She felt the blood drain away from her cheeks.

"Esme, are you okay?"

"No. I don't think I am."

It had to be a trick. Or taken out of context. Her Daddy would never say that about her, would he?

"I'm sure he didn't mean it," said Sophia, but her voice was full of uncertainty.

"Why would someone send this to me?"

"I d-don't know. But Rainer will clear it up, I'm sure of it."

Just then, there was a knock at the door. It was her Daddy, coming to set things straight.

But when she opened the door, it wasn't Rainer. No. It was fate.

The votes didn't take long to come in. Tati manned the booths and ensured everything was above board. The votes were counted and re-counted.

In the end, it was close. Almost too close to call.

"63 votes to 56," Wolf said with a grin on his face as he poured another drink for Rainer. "You beat that fucker by just seven votes!"

Rainer was in a state of shock. As he sat at the table, trying to understand the fact that, by some strange twist of fate — yes, fate — he was now the president of an organization he loved with all his heart, it felt like the world was spinning.

Club members, whether they'd supported him or Dog, were coming up to him and shaking his hand, wishing him well for the future. He could barely keep track of it all.

It was after a full hour of celebration that Dog came up to him.

"Congratulations," he said, with a grim look on his face. "It's a terrible day for the club."

"Never took you for a sore loser," Rainer replied.

"I'm afraid to say that you're the one who's gonna lose big today. You and the rest of the Drifters."

Then, for the last time, he shrugged off his cut, and dropped it to the ground. "Hope your *Little* was worth it." There was something almost malevolent in the way he said it. Something that made Rainer's gut churn. "Have a nice life," Dog said as he walked out of the bar.

"Well, fuck him," Wolf said, grinning. "Another drink?"

"Nah. I need to go check on Esme. Something's not right. I can feel it."

CHAPTER NINETEEN

A S HE DROVE BACK across the city, nightmare scenarios played out in his mind. Esme and Sophia, shot dead on the ground, blood pooling around them. He also had visions of arriving to find the door open, and no-one home.

"It's probably fine. They're probably just fine," he told himself over and over again as he neared his address.

When he arrived at the house, what greeted him was a shock.

The door wasn't open. It was firmly locked. But when he pushed it open, he didn't hear the peals of laughter and fun that he'd been hoping to hear. Instead, there was silence. He took a few more steps inside. "Esme? Sophia?!"

Wolf should be here with him. If his Little was hurt, there would be hell to pay.

He passed by the door to the kitchen and the spare room, but as he approached the lounge door, Rainer heard a vague muffled sound. He didn't have a gun, but he prepared himself for whatever he was about to see.

He kicked open the door and burst in, ready to grab or be grabbed. But there was no need.

"Sophia!" He cried out in shock. She was surrounded by the eviscerated remains of stuffies. There was the skin of teddy bears, horses, and the decapitated head of what was once Om Baby. There was stuffing strewn around, too — a mix of fluffy white fabric, and other, older materials. Maybe even some straw from the very oldest toys.

In the center of it, Sophia sat in one of his chairs, her cheeks streaked with tears. There was a filthy gag in her mouth, and her hands had been taped together with duct-tape. Between them was a walkie-talkie.

Rainer sprung into action, leaping forward and grabbing the gag from between her teeth.

"Rainer," she sobbed. "He's got Esme. I'm sorry, I tried to stop him. But he had a gun."

"No, Sophia, it's not your fault. I'm glad you're safe." Inside, his world was turning upside down. It felt like his heart was about to fall out, like his guts were seizing up. "Who did this?"

Rainer took a knife and started to work on Sophia's bonds. Her wrists had been strapped so tightly that it looked as though the blood supply was being cut off.

"I don't know. Esme seemed to recognize him. She was scared. Really scared. The guy said that if you ever wanted to see Esmeralda alive again, then you should use *that*." She held the walkie-talkie out toward Rainer. He took it.

As he looked at the old-fashioned, boxy piece of plastic, Rainer cycled through who on earth would have done this. It couldn't have been someone in the MC. They'd all been at the election. Plus, Sophia would have recognized him, too. It could have been someone from Esme's past, but he was sure that she would have told him about anyone who might pose a threat to her.

Then, it hit him. The stalker. The guy who the police had taken away.

But how would he have known to come to Rainer's place? Had the guy been watching this whole time? He must have brought the duct-tape because he knew that Sophia was here, too? And why on earth would he have left a walkie-talkie?

"I can't believe this is happening. I can't believe I let the two of you face so much danger. I can't even protect my Little. And I think I should be the fucking president of the club."

Sophia rose from the chair. "It's not your fault, Rainer."

He wanted to work through his options. But he didn't have time. He had to act, right now.

So, he lifted the walkie-talkie to his ear, and clicked the button.

"Whoever this is, you've got my attention."

A voice on the other end of the line replied. "I've got a lot more than that."

Esme had been tied up a bunch of times before. She'd been restrained and strapped down. She'd been held in place and she'd been forced to stay still.

But none of it had ever hurt. And none of it had ever been against her will.

This was different. So, so, so different.

She sat in the dark, looking at the thin crack of light that was her only connection with the outside world. She hoped — she prayed — that soon, somehow, Rainer was going to appear, and he was going to pry those heavy doors open and let her out.

But with every passing minute, her hope was dwindling.

"Please!" she shouted. "I need the bathroom!" It was true. She didn't have some clever escape plan. She just needed to pee, badly. There was no response, so she shouted again, even louder this time. It took a full five minutes of her shouting before someone came to the door.

As the gap cracked open wider and light flooded the shipping container, she squinted, her eyes adjusting to the influx of light.

"Jeez," said the voice of her captor. "Even like this, you look beautiful."

When she'd first seen her stalker, she'd remained mildly optimistic. Maybe he'd come to apologize to her? It hadn't taken long for her to realize that his intentions were far from honorable. He was kidnapping her. And he'd brought a gun. When he forced her outside and she saw that he had help, all hope of getting out of this situation disappeared like snowflakes over a raging fire.

"I need the bathroom," Esme said firmly. She wasn't going to give him the satisfaction of knowing how scared she was.

"I brought it." He lifted a small, plastic tub.

Esme sighed. "Please, just let me go to the bathroom properly."

"Sorry, it's not my decision. Baby, if it were my decision, you'd be on a golden toilet right now."

There was something so pathetic about him. Kevin, he was called. He was a lank, unhealthy-looking mess, with long, greasy hair and small, bloodshot eyes. He'd been so terrified when the police had showed up that she'd honestly thought that she would never see him again.

And yet here she was, captured, in a shipping container.

"Whose decision is it, then?" Her bladder was throbbing.

"My boss. Well, not my boss, exactly. The guy who's been helping me. The guy who wants to see the two of us end up together."

"Kevin, no-one wants that except you."

"You're wrong. He's a good man. A kind man. He wanted to rough you up, but when I told him how special and talented you are, he decided not to."

"He sounds great."

Just then, there was a commotion, and a man who Esme didn't recognize burst into the shipping container. He was carrying a walkie-talkie — the same model as the one Kevin had forced between Sophia's hands.

"Say you're alive." The man sad, gruffly. From the walkie-talkie, she caught snatches of a voice she recognized very well.

"Esme? Sweetheart?"

"Daddy! I'm here! I'm alive! It's Kevin, he t—"

There was a ringing, painful smack as the man with the walkie-talkie slapped her across the face. "Mouth shut, cunt," he said, before wrenching the walkie-talkie away and stepping back outside.

Esme tasted blood. He'd been there — right there on the walkie-talkie, and she hadn't managed to talk to him. How could she be so stupid?

Kevin stepped forward and put the tub down on the ground in front of her. "I know this is horrible for you, sweet thing. But you have to trust me — it's just a little bit of hardship and then we'll be alone together. Forever." He reached inside his dirty denim jacket and pulled out an envelope.

"What's that?" She felt moisture on her chin. Blood trickled down onto the floor.

"Tickets," his eyes widened. "To Costa Rica. For you and me. We'll be gone forever — to paradise. We'll eat lychees and read tarot to one another under the stars."

Esme's pulse pounded. What was going on here? This had to be about more than just her. Who would do something like this to Rainer?

"I'm not going."

The next smile on his lips was sickening. "You are, babygirl. Whether you like it or not. Although I promise, eventually, you'll like it. You'll have no choice." Then he kicked the tub over to her and closed the door.

Darkness enveloped her, then she sobbed like a child.

The instructions were simple. An unrecognizable voice on the walkie-talkie spelled it out for Rainer.

The voice gave him an address — it was a warehouse out of town, near an old zinc mine at North Creek. It was even further out of the city than Albany, but the road was similar. The night was dark, and his lone hog cut an isolated silhouette as he swept toward his destination.

They said he had to come to the address alone, to talk. That was it. Just talk. He couldn't help but feel as though there was something more at stake, though. Something terrible.

Last time he was out here, he was helping to scatter Marcus' ashes. Times were different now. He felt as though he was on his way to another funeral. One that had the potential to be even more life-changing than the first.

The drive was long, and he was anxious the whole way. He had to keep telling himself that if they wanted her dead, she'd be dead already. He'd heard her voice. That had to count for something.

Eventually, he pulled up to the warehouse. In the dark, he could make out almost nothing. Somewhere in the distance, he could have sworn that he made out the sound of engines. Then, the sound stopped.

Showtime.

As he approached, he was met by two men, both with guns, both with grim smiles.

It was only then that he recognized their cuts. Death Division. Fuck. This had just got much, much worse.

He should have grabbed his phone, called in a warning. But, of course, he couldn't. All he could do was pray, and hope that fate had something miraculous in store.

CHAPTER TWENTY

S OMETIMES IN LIFE, IT felt as though you had no control over anything that happened to you. Like you were just a speck of dust caught on the wind.

When Rainer stepped into that warehouse, that was the way he felt. He began to suspect that no matter how he'd acted over the past few weeks, he'd still be right here: looking at his babygirl tied up, feeling as though the club he loved would fall about in tatters, terrified that all of it was because of him.

"You know this isn't the way I wanted it, right?"

He was getting tired of Dog's speeches. He'd been only mildly surprised to see him at the warehouse. As soon as he realized that Dog's motorcycle had been used as some kind of surveillance device, he knew that there were no lengths the man wouldn't go to in order to take control of the Drifters. But only now, when it was staring him in the face, did he understand why.

"It really isn't." The voice came from a TV screen that was mounted on the wall behind Dog. The image on the screen clearly was taken from inside a cell. But it was the plushest, most luxurious prison cell that Rainer had ever seen.

Hank "Whip" Groat. The head of the Death Division Motorcycle Club. He was the reason that the Drifters had been forced out of New York City for ten years. He was the reason that Marcus was scattered across the state right now.

It was all Whip.

"I like you, Rainer," Dog continued.

Rainer couldn't stop looking at Esme. There was blood smudged on her chin, but apart from that, he couldn't see any wounds. If he found out that they'd hurt her there would be hell to pay. Fuck. The thought of it was making him rage inside. It was taking all of his self-control not to just run up to Dog and beat him around the face.

"Yeah, well I think you're a piece of fucking shit."

Dog smiled. "Fair enough. I guess that's fair enough."

"Why don't you just kill him?" That was Whip. He looked like he'd put on some weight in that prison. Rainer thought back to his time inside. He suffered every damn day that he was locked away. Seething with resentment and even guilt — guilt that he'd let himself be taken advantage of in such a heinous way. Clearly, Whip wasn't suffering with guilt. Not at all. Looked like he was living a comfortable, happy life. There had to be lots of sympathetic prisoners in there. People affiliated with the Death Division. And obviously, he had the use of a phone.

Something needed to be done about it.

"I don't want the mess," Dog said. "If you really want me to take over the club, Whip, then this has to be done my way. Exactly as we discussed."

Esme looked terrified. Rainer's mind raced, as he desperately tried to work out the best way out of this situation. It was so, so, so fucked. There was nothing he hated more than feeling powerless.

"What's the point of all this?" Rainer asked.

"The point is," Dog replied, "I'm going to make you an offer that you can't refuse. Just like in the movies. Lucky for you, there ain't even going to be any horse heads involved."

There was some laughter by the other two bikers in the room. Far as Rainer could see, there were only three armed men here. It made him sick — he wouldn't have a chance if he did anything stupid, but he was sure with the amount of adrenaline pumping around his body right now, he could take them in a fair fight.

Of course, this wasn't a fair fight.

"What's your offer?"

"Kevin," Dog said, "hand over the tickets."

Kevin — that was the name of the pathetic stalker who Whip had sprung from prison — looked confused. "The tickets? But... why?"

"Because they don't belong to you."

"B-but, you said I could take my princess to C-Costa Rica."

In that moment, Rainer almost felt sorry for the poor idiot. They'd clearly sent him along to do their dirty work to hide their identity for as long as possible, to maintain plausible deniability. Now that he could see the plan, it had Death Division fingerprints all over it.

"Yeah well, life ain't fair kid. You're not going to Costa Rica with anyone. Just be grateful that you're not going back to prison."

"S-sir, I want my tickets. I need to be with Esme, that's—"

The gunshot was deafening in the enclosed space of the warehouse. Kevin didn't even know he'd been shot – he just hit the ground quietly and stopped talking.

Esme let out a long, haunted scream, the sound fighting its way through her gag.

Dog didn't point the gun at Kevin for too long. A moment later, he let the smoking muzzle drop to his hip.

"Why, Dog?" Rainer asked. He felt the senseless tragedy of the situation acutely. Kevin was an asshole, but no-one deserved to die like that.

"I told you before. I'll do anything to get what I want. Now, Rainer, I trust you're not going to be as dumb as Kevin." Dog gestured to one of the gun-toting goons next to him. The guard walked up to Kevin and pulled an envelope from inside his jacket pocket.

"Take these," Dog said. "Two tickets to Costa Rica. Business class. For you and Esme. And don't come back. Ever."

Rainer was confused. He was genuinely thrown by the offer. "You just want me to leave? What's in it for you?"

"Well. I get to tell the MC that you left the country. I get to say that you *did* love your Little more than your club. I get to be right. That way, I run the club without any suspicion, and the MC can go from strength to strength."

"You mean it can become a chapter of the fucking Death Division?"

There was a dry laugh from the video screen. Groat had lit a cigar and was merrily puffing on it.

"What I do with my club after you leave the country is none of your concern."

Rainer looked at Esme. She was pleading with him, but he couldn't tell what she wanted. Then, she shook her head.

The brave Little thing.

She wanted him to say no, even though she knew it would mean her own life. He had to be brave too.

"What if I say no?" Rainer asked. He hoped that Dog would at least have the patience to answer this question. He'd already proved beyond reasonable doubt that his trigger finger was very, very itchy.

"As I said, it's an offer you can't refuse." Dog said. "Please, don't make me state it again."

Rainer glanced at the windows of the warehouse, as if hoping for divine intervention. He needed time to think, time to hope. Then, he thought of something. Something so dumb and brilliant that he almost smiled.

"I've got a counter-offer," he said.

Dog's eyes narrowed.

She was still looking at Kevin's corpse.

Corpse. Even thinking the word was making her feel detached from reality. She'd never seen a corpse before.

Now, she was looking at a body that just a few hours ago had kidnapped her away from her life and thrown her into chaos.

She should have been happy.

Should she?

Right now, she felt nothing, and it was because of the words that had just come from her Daddy's mouth.

Russian Roulette.

"Here are the rules," Rainer said. Esme could barely process what was happening. Her whole body was trembling as she watched her Daddy speak. "I fire the gun at my temple three times. That gives me a fifty-fifty chance of survival. If I make it, you let me go. I won't bother you again. You'll never hear from me. I'll take Esme and go somewhere far away. Not Costa Rica. I'm staying in the States. But you have my word that I won't bother you."

Was this really his plan?

To risk his life just because he didn't want to live abroad?

Esme couldn't help but think that there had to be some kind of extra, secret plan going on here, but she couldn't think what on earth it could be.

Dog considered. "You really hate Costa Rica that much, huh?"

"I got family here. Don't want to move abroad."

"And you're willing to risk your life for that? Fuck. You're braver than me. Damn. I hope there's no funny business going on here, Rainer. I should say no."

"Wait," the man on the TV screen said. "Humor him. I don't get much entertainment in here. I'd like to watch a man I hate blow his brains out."

"Well, the boss is into the idea," Dog said, sighing. "And you know me. I'm, a people-pleaser." Then, he emptied the barrel of his revolver, and replaced a single bullet. "Let's get this show on the road." The sound the barrel made as he spun it was chilling, like a bone xylophone being rattled with an ivory mallet.

For a moment, it felt as though Esme was hallucinating, like she was watching a smiling skull floating above the room. It was destiny, watching, trying make up its mind about which way to turn.

CHAPTER TWENTY-ONE

Every second of his life had been leading up to this moment. All of it. All the effort his parents had put into raising him. All the laughs and tears he'd shared with friends and enemies. All the motorcycles he'd repaired. All the hours, days, weeks, months he'd spent in prison, seething with hatred and enmity for his brother, the man who put him there. As Rainer looked at the revolver that might take his life, he thought about hate.

It was such a waste. Such a waste of life. Of effort. Of energy.

He'd do anything to have that time back right now. Those endless days, trusting only himself, struggling to see the good in anyone.

Dear Lord, give me that time back and let me spend it with Esme.

Was this the most stupid thing he'd ever done?

Right now, it certainly felt like it. But there was something in the back of his mind, something that Baron had said to him before all this mess had started.

Best way to play Russian Roulette is the best way to play poker. You cheat.

Trouble is, the cheating he had in mind wasn't down to him. It was a matter of trust. And that wasn't a skill that came easy to Rainer.

"Babygirl," he said to Esme. She was looking at him with that pleading expression in her eyes. No doubt she had no idea why on earth he had suggested such a stupid game. It must have seemed like he'd gone mad. He tried to look at her with reassuring eyes, but in truth, there was no guarantee that his plan would work. "I love you. Whatever happens, I need you to know that. I'm doing this for you — for us."

It was true. He hoped that he got the opportunity to prove it.

"Come on," Whip said. "He's stalling, obviously. Looks like big, brave Rainer isn't as big or brave as he pretends to be."

"Now's the time, Rainer. Offer of Costa Rica still stands, otherwise. Or, my *other* offer, which is a game of Russian Roulette played with all six bullets in the chamber."

Rainer looked at the pistol. He had a five-in-six chance of surviving the first pull. They were good odds. Excellent odds. For a moment, he considered turning and pointing the gun at Dog, before frantically pulling the trigger.

It might work, if the bullet was in the first firing chamber. But he couldn't take the chance. Besides, if he shot Dog, the goons would shoot him without missing a beat.

Wait, Rainer. Have faith. Trust.

He knew that his brothers would be close behind him. Sophia would tell Baron what had gone down with Esme, and she'd heard the location on the walkie-talkie too. Maybe he should have stopped to discuss the plan with Baron, but he didn't have a moment to waste. He had to do what he always did with his brothers at the club: trust that they just *got* each other.

"Here goes nothing," he said, stalling. "Never been so good at games of chance." He somehow managed to mask the fear in his voice, as he raised the gun to his temple. The muzzle was warm against his forehead — a memory of the shot that had killed Kevin. Rainer gulped, his throat suddenly dry.

Nearby, he heard a desperate sob from Esme. His eyes flicked to his girl. Would this be the last time he ever saw her beautiful green eyes? Would the last sound he ever heard from her lips be a tortured moan?

Rainer slipped his finger onto the trigger. His heart pounded.

Surely his friends would be here any second?

"Get on with it, asshole!" barked Dog.

Rainer flinched. Was he really going to have to press the trigger?

Suddenly, destiny was on his side, and everything went black.

"What the fuck?!" That was Dog's voice, out ahead. All the lights in the warehouse were out, and the TV screen was dark, too. Even the standby light was off. Clearly, all the power in the warehouse was out.

This was the moment that Rainer had been waiting for.

He felt an urge to spring forward, to throw everything he had at Dog, but he knew that would be a bad idea. Instead, he did what he knew would serve him the best, and he threw himself to the floor.

A moment later, there was the smashing of glass. The sound seemed to come from all around the room, and there was immediate panic from the Death Division.

"What the fuck is happening!?" Dog's voice sounded strangled now. It was wonderful to hear the fear in it.

Rainer could hear Esme, panting with fear around her gag. He hoped she was okay. He started to crawl toward her. He had to reach her, had to reassure her.

It was a moment later that the inevitable happened. One of the bikers called out: "Use your phone flashlights!" Rainer heard an acceleration of something from nearby, and, a moment later, when the lights *did* flick on, he heard screams.

Because there were people in here with them.

Baron, Wolf, and Crank. The three men wore outlandish visors — night-vision equipment that the club had requisitioned years ago, finally put to good use. The Death Division didn't have a chance. The Drifters were already in place, and they started to choke out the thugs who'd been holding Esme to ransom.

Rainer reached his Little and grabbed the gag, yanking it out of her mouth. "Darling, it's okay. Everything's going to be just fine." Beams of white light played over the space as the Death division jerked against the strength of the Drifters. There was just enough light for him to find Esme's lips and press his own against them.

Something pulled him out of the moment, though. A roar of defiance and rage. Dog was off, sprinting for the exit — he knew that he was in serious, serious trouble.

Rainer glanced at Baron, Wolf, and Crank — they were all busy apprehending the other Death Division members. But there was no way that he was going to let Dog get away. Not this time. "Wait here. You're safe now," Rainer said to Esme. Then, he got up, and he ran.

Outside, it was almost entirely dark. The stars up above were the only source of light, and it was virtually impossible to see. Rainer felt like a hunter as he traced the sound that Dog made in the darkness. He heard gravel, and then, as he got further away from the warehouse, the sound of branches underfoot.

Fuck, he'd gone into the forest.

As Rainer passed the wooded threshold, he took out his phone and flashed it between the trees. He saw a shadow in the dark, darting away from him. His heart pounded when he thought about what this bastard had put Esme through, and what he'd almost put the club through, too.

"I'm coming for you, traitor!" Rainer shouted out, not caring if he gave away his position.

It was a mistake, though. A terrible one.

As he kept running forward, there was another roar, and he felt the weight of a body slam into him from the side. It was Dog — he'd been waiting in ambush for him. Rainer was down on his back, with something hard — a tree root, maybe — pressing up against him, causing him agony as Dog pushed him down.

He felt punches. One, two, three of them, each harder than the last. There was a sickening crunch as the last connected with his nose. But somehow, miraculously, no pain. That would come later, no doubt.

No, right now, the only thing that Rainer felt was pure, unadulterated adrenaline. He pushed up, and as he somehow fought to get to his feet, Dog yelped, tumbling backward. Now it was Rainer's turn — he found Dog's face with his fists, connecting over and over again. Dog cried out in pain, but Rainer couldn't stop. He wasn't just punching him because of the hurt he'd caused to Esme — it was so much more than that.

It was because, once again, Rainer had trusted him — trusted that Dog wasn't a bad guy, just had a different vision for the club. But he'd been deceived. And the more he punched, the more he realized that he wasn't just hitting Dog — he was punching his brother too.

That's what stayed his hand.

He looked down and saw his brother's face looking back up at him — puffy and vulnerable and in unspeakable pain. But still his brother. Still his blood. And he stopped.

"It's over, Dog," Rainer said, reaching down and squeezing his enemy's shoulder. "It's over."

CHAPTER TWENTY-TWO

TWO WEEKS LATER

T HE PAST TWO WEEKS had been a blur. Rainer had almost constantly been *with* people. Club members, prospects, Littles, even the goddamn police. It had felt as though he hadn't even had a moment to himself, let alone much time to spend with the one person he actually wanted to be with right now: Esme.

Finally, he had a moment to himself.

"I wish I didn't have to do this."

His Little girl's eyes were wide and soft. That electric green took on so many different personae. There were times when she was the sexiest woman in the world — eyes glinting with the promise of pleasure and submission. There were times when she was unbelievably adorable — pools of green sparkling with excitement at the thought of doing something as simple as coloring in or watching cartoons. Then, there were times like now, when the emotion in her emerald-green eyes was supportive and loving, and there was no one in the world who could match her tenderness.

"I know, Daddy. I'm gonna miss you too. But it's like you said —
this is important."

"Right. And you've got plans, anyway. I shouldn't put this off."

"I love you, Daddy."

"You *and* Om Baby?"

This prompted Esme to pull Om Baby out of her bag. You wouldn't
be able to tell that, just a couple weeks ago, Om Baby's head had been
ripped clean off her body. Sophia was a professional, after all.

"Om Baby loves you too. But my feelings for you are a little bit
different to Om Baby's." There was that sexy expression that he loved
so much.

Rainer leaned in and kissed Om Baby on the head. Then, he leaned
past the stuffie, and kissed Esme on the mouth. She responded instantly to his demands. Their kisses had been intense right from the
start, but as they'd started to learn even more about each other's bodies, it was almost like they were a musical band, playing together in
perfect rhythm.

He was the drummer, dictating the pace, demanding that Esme
followed his lead. But she was the singer, adding beautiful flourishes
to the piece they performed together. She fought to keep up with his
tongue, she caressed his body as he gripped hers, she ran hands through
his hair as he gripped the fleshy goodness of her ass.

She sighed as they parted, and he kissed her again on the top of the
head.

"Remember," he said, "I want to know when you're heading home.
You're to stay safe, understand?" It wasn't that he was truly worried
about her, but his protective streak had gotten even wider since the
business with Kevin and Dog. And now that he was acting president
of the Drifters, he felt even more of a duty to keep every single Little
on the planet safe.

"Yes Daddy. You know I'm a good girl. You can trust me."

"I know, sugar. It's not you — it's the rest of the world I'm worried about."

Then, the moment came, and they parted.

A second later, Rainer's phone buzzed in his pocket. He picked it out. It was a message... from Esme.

Miss you, Daddy.

He turned and looked at her. She grinned, and ran towards him, before squeezing herself up against his body. He squeezed back, chuckling at her fierce, fierce love. It was a feeling he never wanted to lose.

To his surprise, on the way to the penitentiary, he'd called Wolf.

"Hey, Prez," his friend said. Rainer was sat on the subway. He wasn't one for talking in public much, but this felt like an exception he was going to have to make. "You on the way to the big house?"

"Mmmhmm. I'd say it's been too long, but honestly, I could do without seeing the inside of a cell for many years." Around him, people glanced nervously at him. He probably cut quite an imposing figure. A big, heavily-tattooed biker, talking about prison. His face was still somewhat swollen from the pounding he'd received in the woods. Mind you, Dog's face was quite a bit worse.

"You call for a pep-talk?"

"Actually, I was hoping to chat to your Little girl."

"Sophia? Sure."

There was a rustle, and Wolf handed the phone over.

"Hey darlin', how you doing?"

"Good thank you, Mister President." She giggled.

"I was hoping for some advice."

She laughed. "From me? Um, let me think." Then, she said in a gruff voice, clearly pretending to be Baron, "A falling knife has no handle."

"Well, that's good advice, but I was hoping for something specific. You went to visit your father in prison, didn't you?"

Sophia's father was a mob boss who'd tried repeatedly but unsuccessfully, to force her to marry Whip. After his final attempt, he'd ended up in prison — the cops finally having enough evidence to convict him.

"I did."

"What was it like? Did you forgive him?"

"No. I didn't. I told him that he was out of my life."

Rainer nodded. "Smart, after what he did to you."

"I decided that I could live without him. Not everyone would make the same decision, though."

"Yeah. I'm on my way for a different reason."

"Good luck," Sophia said. "Just... keep what serves you."

Keep what serves you. It was good advice. But Rainer felt as though he'd already lost something, and he hoped, desperately, that he could get it back.

Esme knew that she had to do this. She just didn't know why it felt so hard.

Green-Wood cemetery was a sprawling, strange space in Brooklyn. Famous people were buried here, but there were also spaces available for people with the money and connections to make it happen.

It was also the final resting place of her sister, Rowan.

Esme hadn't been here for many, many years. In fact, the last time she'd been here had been at her sister's funeral. She remembered the day clearly — it was the first funeral she'd ever been to. It was over-whelmingly sad, and she spent the whole day crying.

Today, however, she didn't feel as though she was going to cry.

She stepped through the entrance arch and was struck by how beautiful this place was. Her folks had spent a huge amount of money finding Rowan a spot. A traditional casket burial would have been too rich, even for their means, so they'd had Rowan cremated first, before finding a smaller plot for her.

Esme kept going over this information in her head. She had done for years, mainly because she was sure that if it had been her to die, her parents wouldn't have fought hard for a burial in a picturesque ceme-tery. It was a privilege that only her perfect sister would be offered.

Today though, she didn't feel angry at her parents. And for the first time, maybe ever, she didn't feel angry with herself.

She'd planned the route around the cemetery in advance, just like Daddy had taught her to. In the past, she'd have just turned up and hoped that she found the right plot. Not anymore, though. The new Esme didn't leave anything to chance.

Past ancient tombs and marble mausoleums, past headstones and flowers and countless other symbols of grief. Crosses and rosaries, statuettes of Christ and small, orthodox icons.

It was a far cry from the ritual items that Esme used for her tarot readings, but something about the situation put her in that deep, meditative mood.

Eventually, she found it. A small, unremarkable headstone. She knew that somewhere beneath the earth were her sister's mortal re-mains. Just ash, most definitely 'gone' now. It was strange to think that the most real, tangible remains of her sister were the memories of her that she still had.

The headstone was green marble, with white veins running through it.

Rowan Adams, 1998-2012. Beloved daughter and sister.

It was almost nothing really. Five words for a whole life.

"Ro," Esme said, sighing a little as she spoke. "I haven't visited in a long time. I'm sorry."

The sun, which had been hidden behind clouds this morning, broke out, casting long shadows behind the gravestones and trees which surrounded them.

"I wanted to come see you because I miss you. When I think about the person you would be today... it just kills me. And I wanted to say sorry. I don't blame myself for your death anymore. I don't blame anyone except the man who hit you. But I wanted to say sorry because I haven't been honoring your life. I've been doing nothing, hiding behind fear and self-hatred. I've let my talent and ambition shrivel away. But I'm here to say that I'm stopping that now."

Esme held up her hand to her heart, closing her eyes.

"From this moment on, I'm going to live, Rowan. And you'll be with me, living inside me, seeing all the wonders that life has to offer. That's my promise to you."

As she breathed in and out, she felt warmth, light, forgiveness on the breeze. For a moment, she considered throwing her arms around the gravestone, embracing the piece of rock.

But it was pointless. It wasn't her sister. Her sister was inside *her*, wrapped around her heart, beating in time to the rhythm of possibility.

"Rowan," she said, finally succumbing to tears, "what I wouldn't give to see your smile one more time."

Then, across the breeze, she heard something, she was sure of it. *Smile for me.*

He'd forgotten just how much like him his brother looked.

When they'd been kids, people had asked if they'd been twins. Course, that used to drive Rainer nuts, seeing as he was the older one. Tuco had loved it.

Now, sitting across from his brother, a pane of safety glass between them, many years later, it wasn't like looking in a mirror, not at all. It was more like looking through a portal into a parallel universe. If Rainer hadn't been released from prison, this could well be how his life would have ended up.

Rainer looked at the wrinkles on his brother's face — so much deeper and more severe than the ones on his. Tuco's hair was graying even faster than his, and he had facial tattoos — tears and spiders' webs, as well as Roman numerals that Rainer couldn't decipher.

Fuck.

It had been years.

"Brother," he said eventually.

"Rainer. Surprised to see you." He sounded like someone who smoked about a hundred cigarettes a day. That was probably not far from the truth.

"Surprised to be here."

He was doing it. Somehow, he was speaking to Tuco without anger. It was as though he'd been cleansed, as though the trauma of his brother's betrayal had finally left him.

"You here to see the sights?" Tuco grinned, and it took Rainer back in time. He hadn't seen that expression on his brother's face since they were kids. Before the drugs, before the loss, before the struggle.

"No. Not here to see the sights. Here for something else."

"Truth is," Tuco said, "I been waiting a long time to see you."

Rainer knew it was true. Everyone now and then — once a year or so — a representative of the state penitentiary system would reach out and tell him that his brother wanted to see him. He would politely decline.

"Hope it's worth the wait," Rainer smiled wryly.

"Oh, it is." His brother's sincerity shocked him. "It really is. This whole time I've been in here, I've been desperate to see you. Desperate to tell you just how sorry I am."

"You apologizing?"

His brother's eyes were wet with tears, their rims red. "I am. You don't have to accept. I ge—"

"I accept." Rainer said, quickly. "More than that. I forgive you. I understand. We were kids. You were dumb." He breathed in deep. "I'm sorry for what you've been through. I'm sorry you don't have your freedom. I'm sorry for it all."

Tuco pushed a palm up onto the safety glass, and Rainer did the same.

"I missed you so much."

"I missed you to." It was good to admit it. As soon as he said the words, his heart felt light, his soul felt free. "Fuck, Tuco, I got a lot of shit to catch you up on."

"Might not have time." Tuco glanced at the clock.

"Well, I guess I'll have to come back."

CHAPTER TWENTY-THREE

T HE SAGE HAD BEEN burned. The lights had been dimmed. Candles were lit — black ones, of course. Offerings to the dark gods of fate had been placed on an altar — handcuffs, silk, and chocolate.

"Didn't think I'd be getting another tarot reading after the last one," Rainer said. They were at Esme's place. It was now unrecognizable, of course. Not a single misplaced item of clothing, no molding old plates, and there were no scraps of paper or receipts to be seen anywhere. Where there used to be mess, was the order of a life lived in control, and to the plan.

"Well, my willing subject, this is a very, *very* different draw to a normal tarot reading." Esme was wearing an outfit that made her feel extremely sexy. A deep black corset, rimmed with red silk. A short, velvet skirt, revealing fishnet stockings over her pale skin. She'd even invested in a jet-black shawl, which covered her hair, as well as a headband adorned with small gold coins. If there was a personification of sexy fate, she was it. This was a special day, and she'd decided to make it extra special for her Daddy.

Later on, Rainer was going to be officially sworn in as President
of the Drifters. He'd have to take an oath, swear on the rules of the
club, and then — probably — have to make some kind of speech.
She wanted to make sure that he was as relaxed and confident as was
humanly possible.

So, she'd bought something very, very special for him.

"Yeah, I don't remember you being quite so... sexy last time we did
this."

"So, you think that Lady Luck is sexy, do you? How insolent."

Rainer grinned, clearly enjoying Esme's silly roleplay. "Sorry, Lady
Luck. You have my apologies." Then, under his breath, he added, "You
filthy wench."

She pretended not to hear the second part. "Very good. Apology
accepted. Now, we will begin the reading." Esme took out the deck.
She'd not yet even had a chance to fully look through this special deck
she'd bought. Hopefully it would be as good as all the reviews online
said it was.

"Wait, what's the picture on the..." Rainer's voice trailed off as he
caught sight of the art on the backs of the cards. It was a very erotic
painting of a sub, naked, with her wrists strapped together. There was
a riding crop resting against her plump, spankable bottom.

"Don't question the fates," Esmeralda snapped, "or the magic may
not flow." She was really getting into character now, absolutely loving
the feeling of mystery and dark eroticism that was moving over her.

"I won't question. I'll just... study the image... carefully."

"Naughty Daddy!" Esme couldn't help but say. "Now, you're normally the one handing out the rules, but today, it's my job as Lady
Luck to make sure you know how this will be played. In this deck
are a series of... sexy tasks. Since I am your ever-serving sub, I agree to
the whim of the cards. Whatever is printed on these extremely magical

items, you have my permission to enact on me." Her heart beat faster as she saw Rainer's eyebrow rise.

"What an interesting idea."

"We will leave my punishment to the whims of the fates."

The atmosphere was changing, becoming thick with possibility. She looked into his eyes, and he looked right back, holding her gaze, unblinking, completely focused on her.

"Agreed. I won't hold back, Lady Luck, if that's what you want."

"That's what I demand."

She shuffled the deck, the big cards difficult to handle, but she managed for Daddy.

Soon, she had five cards. She lay them out on the tarot mat, taking her time with each one, making Rainer wait, just the way he liked to make her wait for her pleasure.

"The two final cards are linked," she explained. "We need to do this one before this one. Okay?"

He nodded.

"So, Daddy, which one are you gonna turn over first?"

Now, he had the power. This felt good. Comfortable.

For a moment, he hovered over a couple of the cards, making her wait, then, he picked up the middle one, and turned it over. There, in the middle of the card, was a single sentence, written in elegant, looping cursive.

Spank your sub's bottom five times with the sole of your shoe.

Esme gasped and bit her lip. Spanked with the sole of a shoe. No-one had ever done that to her before.

"Did you stack this deck, Little Girl? Seems like you got lucky with the first punishment."

"Lady Luck never cheats, Daddy," Esme said.

"Pull up your skirt, sub," Rainer ordered, suddenly all business. "I wanna see that perfect ass of yours."

"Yes sir," Esme said. She rose from her seat, turned her back to Rainer, and tugged her skirt up. It was tight, and the stockings underneath rode up with it, pulling them tight over the soft flesh of her thighs.

"Good girl," he said. She felt his hard fingers grip her buttock, and she gasped when he squeezed hard. "Remember, I'm in charge of these punishments. I'm in control of how hard you get spanked, and where precisely I choose to spank you."

"Yes sir," she breathed, scarcely able to hide her excitement. In anticipation of a good, hard fucking, she wasn't wearing any panties, and she felt the wetness of her pussy dripping down her leg.

Rainer gripped her shoulder and pulled her down over the table. Her cheek smushed into the card printed with the spanking forfeit — it was right there, next to her eye. Esme heard Rainer slip off his shoe, and then, a moment later, she felt its cold hardness resting on her bottom.

"You know, if you didn't love this so much, I'd feel a lot worse about the pain I'm about to inflict on you."

She didn't even have time to react before the spanks came. He aimed each one carefully, hitting the top and bottom of each buttock, and then spanking once across the middle, catching half of each cheek perfectly.

It was so fast, so hard, so painful that it took her breath away. It felt a little like being spanked with a paddle, but there was an extra agony in the pattern on the sole of the shoe.

"That looks pretty, Little one," Rainer said. "Your pale skin's pinkening up, Lady Luck."

"My destiny is to serve you, Master."

"Good. Then pull your skirt down and turn over the next card."

She did exactly what he asked, wincing with pain as she parked her butt back down on the chair. "Daddy, that feels so good. Why does it feel so dang good?"

"It feels good cause you're a little kinkster, Esme," he smiled. "Kinked and bent into the sweetest, sexiest shape I've ever seen. Now hurry up and turn over the next card."

It wasn't just her butt cheeks that were blushing.

Rainer pointed at the next card in a row, and Esme tensed up. She wondered what was coming next. Then, she turned it over.

Blindfold your sub. The blindfold remains for the rest of the game.

"How will I turn over the cards?" Esme asked.

"Don't worry, I'm sure we can work something out." Rainer opened a drawer nearby. It was Esme's 'naughty drawer.' Within it were a variety of sex toys, including blindfolds and manacles. "I wonder which one I'm gonna pick," Rainer mused, as he surveyed the options available to him.

Esme trembled as he brought the blindfold over to her — a simple, black silk band which he tied around her head until it was nice and snug.

"Can't see anything?"

"Not a thing, Daddy."

"Good. Time for the next card." She loved how he took control of the situation. Even though she'd set it all up, he was such a natural Dom that he couldn't help but take the lead. He gripped her slim fingers in his big hand and moved them over another card.

"That one?" she asked.

"Mmhmm," he replied. She wondered what he looked like right now. It struck her that if he wanted to, he could just make up whatever he wanted for the text of the card. It also struck her that Rainer would never, in a million years, lie about something like that.

"Oh, that's interesting." Rainer sounded genuinely surprised.

"What does it say, Daddy?"

"It says: *Make your sub come just using your cock. You can't fuck her with it.*"

Esme felt her heart quicken. He was going to be touching her with his cock. She hadn't dreamed that things would progress so fast. She barely had time to respond before she felt Rainer's strong hand around her arms. She gasped at the ease with which he lifted her, then felt lost in him as he stretched her out on the table.

"That's it, babygirl, open up those legs for Daddy."

"Do you want me to take my stockings off?"

"Daddy decides what happens."

Then, she felt it, the weight and heat of his cock, as he let it rest on her thigh. It almost felt like she could feel his manhood in high definition. She tried to breathe through the lust, but it was impossible, and she knew that she was getting wetter with each passing second.

"You're so fucking sexy, you know that?" His voice was close to her, she felt his breath on her skin. "I wish I was allowed to fuck you right now. But that would be cheating."

She shuddered as she felt him drag his thick cock up her soft skin, and then, she let out a gasp as he let it weigh heavily on her pussy.

"D-Daddy," she panted, "That feels good."

"You're so wet," he remarked. "So wet for me."

He started to slowly slide his cock up and down, pushing the tip gently over her entrance, then squeezing his length against her. The thought of what he was doing made her feel faint.

"H-holy heck, oh my, Daddy..." The blindfold was making it so much more intense. She imagined what he might look like right now.

"Do you know how hard it is not to push my cock in you?"

She started to tremble as she felt her pleasure grow. "Please Daddy, do it." She bit her lip, and felt her eyes roll back.

"I'm saving you for later." He pushed his cock down flat against her clit. "Now come for Daddy, babygirl."

Esme didn't need to be told twice. It was a swirling, multicolored orgasm, as her brain painted vivid spurts of light against the insides of her eyelids. Her body shook, and she grabbed the sides of the table as she submitted to the sensation.

"Time for the linked cards," he panted, "First one says: *Apply liberal lubricant to your sub's asshole.*"

Esme felt the color drain from her cheeks. She'd never done anal before. Clearly Rainer picked up on this.

"We don't have to do it," he said. "I can pick two more cards. I don't mind. I want you to be comfortable."

She gripped his arm. "No, Daddy, I want to do it. I want you to be my first." Then, she added, "And your last."

It's hard to describe, but she could hear the smile as Rainer said, "Sounds peachy to me."

Rainer flipped Esme over on the table. She didn't watch Rainer find the lube, but she heard it. She didn't observe the lube drip down onto her behind, but when her Daddy started to massage it rhythmically into her other opening, she sure as hell felt it.

He started gently, pushing the button of her opening with a soft fingertip. Then, he worked carefully, methodically, like he was working as an artisan, perfectly stretching her opening. He knew what was going to have to fit.

As he worked, he used another finger on her clit, massaging her, making sure that she stayed in that pleasure place.

When his finger slipped in, she was ready for it. The sensation was strange, at once uncomfortable and deeply, deeply pleasurable. She moaned as he pushed in farther, trembling at the thought of what was to come. He took a moment to wash his hands and then it was time for the next card.

"*Fuck your sub's ass.*" He read the text to her. She knew it had been coming, and the anticipation for it felt like a mountain in front of her, a mountain that she was going to have to climb.

"I'm going to be a good girl for you, Daddy," she panted, as she felt the smooth tip of his cock between her legs.

"A good girl? This isn't something you're just gonna take, baby. By the time I'm done with you, you're gonna be begging for more."

And then, he pushed against her opening, and he was in. It took a while for him to work the full, enormous length of himself into her. He thrust in and out slowly, with great control, as she panted and moaned with the all-encompassing sensation of it all.

"This was your destiny, Esme. To get fucked in the ass by Daddy."

"I like it," she panted, pictures of Rainer's clenched jaw in her mind. "I'm yours to do what you want with."

The further he pushed, the better it started to feel, until she realized that it felt really, *really* fucking good. It was like his cock was pushing against her pussy from the inside out, and when he took a finger and pushed it against her clit, it was like fireworks burst in her brain.

"Oh my god, oh my fucking god!" she shrieked as he fucked her harder, as he claimed her mind, body, and soul.

"You want Daddy to come in that tight little ass, don't you?"

"Pleeasssee," she moaned, as another, deeper orgasm took hold of her.

In a moment of pure, animalistic lust, Rainer took hold of her thighs and pulled them back, wedging his cock as far into her body as he could. Then, she felt his lips on her as he finally, unstoppably, emptied his seed inside her.

"Holy fuck," she moaned as she began to see stars.

"Don't think you can cuss just because I've got my cock in your ass."

He removed the blindfold and flipped her over. He was smiling. She smiled back.

And for a moment, it felt as though the whole damn universe smiled with them.

CHAPTER
TWENTY-FOUR

T HEY CALLED IT A coronation. It was dumb really. Rainer wasn't a king. He wasn't royalty. He was just like the rest of them: a biker who cared about his MC.

Course, he felt a *little* like a king. He had just fucked the ass of a princess, after all.

"He's our new president. Only the second in the history of the club." Tatiana was doing a good job of bigging him up. He'd had a brief chat with her before the coronation, and he was happy to have her by his side.

Tatiana was pleased to help with the administrative side of the club. She'd be able to organize new prospects and help with the logistics of planning trips and charity events. If — of course — that was what the club decided that it wanted to do.

He had other plans, too, but those plans wouldn't be discussed until the big ride.

"Now, I pass you over to Rainer Ortiz."

There were cheers, claps, and laughter as Rainer took the stage. He took a moment to look out at the crowd of his brothers. He'd never wanted this. Never thought for a moment that he'd be Prez.

As he scanned through the crowd, he saw the Little table, where Esme, Sophia, Molly, and the others sat. There were half a dozen of them, but he hoped that soon, with a pro-Little agenda, they'd recruit more to the Little Drifters. Anyway, that was for the future.

So much was for the future.

"I don't got much to say," he said, scratching his head. "I want what's best for this club, but I'm not an oracle. I don't know what fate's got in store. I'm only making one executive decision as President of this club. We're going on a ride. A long one. All of us, we're gonna need to take time off work. We need to put the rest of our lives on hold. We're going down south, almost like a vision quest. Together, we're gonna make big decisions about this club, and what we want from it."

He could feel the excitement growing as the rest of the members smiled and chatted amongst themselves.

"I don't know what the future holds, but what I do know is, with you boys and girls behind me, it's going to be epic!"

More cheers. More laughter. And somewhere, nearby, he felt it: Marcus, watching with pride, wishing them the best, wishing them happiness.

It was later that night that he walked in on her. Esme, head down, feet high up in the sky. She was straight as an arrow, perfectly in balance. Strong, supple, completely in control.

He could hear her breathing, could see her sweat. There she was: his fate, his destiny, his choice.

Thanks so much for reading!

Head over here to read a bonus epilogue featuring Rainer and Esme!

And if you haven't read my Daddies MC series yet, get on it!

Plus... keep in touch!

*Don't forget to find me on **Facebook**! And join my **readers' group** for maximum Lucky fun!*

Lucky x

*P. S. I loved writing this book! I really focused on creating a tight plot, and I loved how the characters had completely different ideas about destiny, and yet they were fated to be together. Also, I've recently been getting into tarot myself and I loved having Esme give the other characters tarot readings. So much fun! Also, as always, I took wicked pleasure in creating the kinky scenes and the suspense. If you enjoyed reading this book as much as I enjoyed writing it, please **give me a review**! Every review means so much to me! It helps me see what's working, see what I can improve, and most importantly of all, helps me keep doing the thing I love. :)*

Also By Lucky Moon

DADDY SAVES CHRISTMAS (IN A LITTLE COUNTRY
CHRISTMAS)

SECOND CHANCE DADDIES

DADDY'S GAME

THE DADDY CONTEST

DADDY'S ORDERS

DRIFTERS MC

DADDY DEMANDS

DADDY COMMANDS

DADDY DEFENDS

DADDIES INC

BOSS DADDY

YES DADDY

COLORADO DADDIES

HER WILD COLORADO DADDY

FIERCE DADDIES

THE DADDIES MC SERIES

DANE

ROCK

HAWK

DADDIES MOUNTAIN RESCUE

MISTER PROTECTIVE

MISTER DEMANDING

MISTER RELENTLESS

SUGAR DADDY CLUB SERIES

PLATINUM DADDY

CELEBRITY DADDY

DIAMOND DADDY

CHAMPAGNE DADDY

LITTLE RANCH SERIES

DADDY'S FOREVER GIRL

DADDY'S SWEET GIRL

DADDY'S PERFECT GIRL

DADDY'S DARLING GIRL

DADDY'S REBEL GIRL

MOUNTAIN DADDIES SERIES

TRAPPED WITH DADDY

LOST WITH DADDY

SAVED BY DADDY

STUCK WITH DADDY

TRAINED BY DADDY

GUARDED BY DADDY

STANDALONE NOVELS

PLEASE DADDY

DDLG MATCHMAKER SERIES

Copyright

Printed in Great Britain
by Amazon

29442787R00129